The Wayward Son

By Gary Robinson

DEDICATION

This book is dedicated to ending human trafficking.

ABOUT THE AUTHOR

I write books with the purpose of elevating the human condition. Please follow me @Grobinbooks on Twitter. At the time of this printing, my website GaryRobinsonBooks.com and IamAgainstHumanTrafficking.org are currently under construction.

The Wayward Son

1

Tanner took a deep breath and wiped the sweat and blood from his right eye with his forearm. He stood in his corner, shifting his weight from one leg to another. Aimee, Tanner's coach and sister, stepped in front of him, placed a hand on his shoulder, and leaned towards him. His eye was beginning to swell. She quickly applied a cotton swab soaked with adrenaline to Tanner's eye. When she finished wiping the blood from his face, she pulled a tube of Vaseline from her sweatpants and squeezed a quarter-sized amount onto her index finger. She rubbed the gel over the cut and wiped one last time with her thumb to clean off any excess. Aimee then stepped back and pointed her index finger at her chest. She repeated the gesture several times and then placed her index finger and thumb together near her navel, and pulled her fingers up towards her chest, like she was zipping a jacket. She then placed her index finger at the side of her head and turned her finger out and towards Tanner.

A confident smile filled his face.

His sister was proud of him.

No one expected Tanner to be a relevant competitor in this boxing tournament, but he was three minutes away from making it to the championship round. Tanner had studied all his opponents in great detail and had won every fight decisively. Tanner waved Aimee closer. He shouted into her ear, "War Chief never trains. Look at him!" He pointed towards his opponent.

Aimee glanced over quickly and returned her attention to her brother and nodded.

"I'm surprised a cigarette isn't hanging from his mouth. He is always smoking. I'll just wear him down some more and then finish him," Tanner said assuredly.

Aimee made a fist, and then pointed at her eyes.

He nodded, "Oh, yeah, I'm going after his eyes!"

She slapped his left shoulder for encouragement and stepped out of the ring.

Tanner stared at his opponent, War Chief, whose trainer was attending to him. The South Central Los Angeles street fighter was a physical specimen. He towered over every other fighter and his muscular physique evoked intimidation. He was breathing heavily and being treated for two swollen eyes. His man bun was almost completely disheveled, and his long hair was nearly covering his face. His trainer, with a sense of urgency, attempted to fasten the hair unsuccessfully.

Tanner took a deep breath and smiled. He was one round away from fighting for the heavyweight championship. The weeklong contest had started with sixty-four fighters from around the world. The red-headed farmer's son from West Texas had defeated four other contestants on his way to this semi-final bout. The daily five-round matches were taking their toll on the boxers.

War Chief pushed aside his trainer, stood up, and scowled at Tanner. The red-colored grease under his eyes started to run.

Tanner chuckled nervously, punched his gloves together, and then the bell rang.

The Las Vegas arena crowd was on their feet shouting. He could feel the vibration underneath him. War Chief walked fearlessly to Tanner and swung wildly with both hands.

The young fighter ducked and stepped back. The Chief, between heavy breaths, laughed loudly as he chased the smaller fighter around the boxing ring.

Tanner moved away just far enough to ensure that

War Chief's violent swings missed hitting him. He stepped forward to provoke his opponent and then moved backwards to lean away or duck under his violent throws.

War Chief quickly tired and started to stumble. He tried to grab Tanner and force him to stay in his clutches, but he no longer had the speed or stamina to catch him. Soon, War Chief leaned over and placed his gloves on his thighs and panted for air.

Tanner quickly looked at Aimee.

She nodded and began to silently laugh.

Tanner punched the top of War Chief's head. He attempted to stand but was met with a combination of blows to his face. One hand was on his knee to keep him from falling, and the other was flailing helplessly in the air. Tanner stepped in and hit him with an uppercut to one of his swollen eyes. He hit him several more times in the temple when the referee jumped in front of him waving his arms to call the fight.

Tanner had defeated War Chief, the tournament's #2 ranked fighter, and handed him the first loss of his professional career.

Aimee rushed to Tanner and gave him a hug, but her joy soon turned to concern when she looked at her brother's bruised face. She grabbed his hand, but Tanner motioned her to wait. He tilted his head backwards to signal her to look behind him.

The ring was beginning to fill with people.

Aimee's mouth dropped in amazement, and Tanner couldn't stop smiling at her. He turned to face the oncoming cameras. Aimee released her brother's hand and stepped back; she wasn't prepared for this. She only trusted her brother, and she hated it when her condition made others feel awkward or overly sympathetic. Tanner reached for his sister's hand but to no avail. He turned away from the cameras and desperately looked for her amongst the growing crowd entering the ring.

Aimee stood watching her brother and knew he was worried. She lifted her hand above the crowd that separated them, and pushing people aside, Tanner took his sister's hand. He pulled her into the center of the ring as she tried to hide behind his right shoulder.

The emcee announced: "Ladies and gentlemen, by technical knockout, and on his way to the biggest fight of his life. To be seen here at the lovely Babylon Casino and Hotel in downtown Las Vegas on Saturday night. He will fight for the championship of the first annual United States Boxing League Ring of Champions tournament. The winner takes the ten-million-dollar prize home!"

The arena crowd roared. Aimee squeezed Tanner's wrist tightly.

The emcee continued: "Your winner, Tanner Childress."

Tanner raised one arm humbly in the air, then brought it back down and looked at his sister and confidently nodded. She shook her head and laughed

quietly. With an unspoken word, they both understood the

magnitude of this moment. All the long hours of training,

studying, and dreaming were close to being rewarded.

2

Tanner lifted his hand above his eyes to minimize the glare from camera flashes. Reporters from around the world filled the casino convention room. Aimee was sitting to Tanner's right, and the colorful boxing promoter, Midas, with wild, unkempt, gray hair, wearing a purple silk suit with a broad grin, sat to his left. Tanner's challenger, only known as "Kaine," sat at the end of the table. He looked angry and annoyed surrounded by his entourage of trainers and supporters, who were equally annoyed and silent.

A reporter continued questioning the young boxer, "Las Vegas oddsmakers have you as a heavy underdog, Tanner. Do you think you have a puncher's chance to beat Kaine?"

Tanner smiled and leaned over the table to look at his opponent, purposely trying to poke fun at Kaine. Tanner nodded and said, "I don't think I'll have any trouble."

Kaine slammed his fist on the table and grunted, "Huh!"

Another reporter attempted to ask Tanner a question. Instead, Kaine now slammed both his fists onto the table, which knocked over the glass of water and the centerpiece stationed in front of him. A few of Kaine's team members hurried to clean the spilled water covering the table and dripping to the carpeted floor.

Kaine pointed his finger at Tanner, turned to face the audience, and shouted, "Don't waste your time asking this clown any questions. When I'm finished with him, if he survives, he will be eating out of a straw for the rest of his life!"

Aimee held Tanner's hand. It was her way to comfort him. He turned and whispered, "Trust me. He becomes careless when he gets angry."

Kaine then stood and screamed, "Who is this guy, anyway? Have you heard of him before this tournament? No! And when this tournament is over, and they carry his ass out on a gurney, you will forget his name. He's nothing but a redneck hillbilly from West Texas."

Tanner clutched his glass of water tightly.

Kaine shouted another insult at his challenger, "He may be the only one in his hometown that has all of his teeth."

Kaine's entourage started to clap and encourage the boxer to continue.

"Look at his manager and trainer . . . " Kaine

pointed at Tanner.

Tanner's face turned red; he tried to calm himself by drinking from his glass of water. He finished his drink but continued to clutch his glass.

Kaine incessantly berated him, "And whatever else she does for him. I wouldn't be surprised if they have cross-eyed children together."

Kaine suddenly ducked backwards to avoid the pint glass that whizzed by his head and shattered into pieces against the wall.

Tanner headed directly towards Kaine, his face was fiery red, and the veins in his temples were pulsed.

The promotor stepped in front of a charging Tanner, but Midas looked into the boxer's eyes and could see death. He mumbled quietly, "Good Lord," and stepped away from him.

Kaine's eyes widened as he tried to assess the situation, glancing at his crew, the nearest exit, and into

Tanner's eyes. Several of his entourage formed a wall in front of Kaine, holding their arms out and palms opened against Tanner's chest and shoulders. "Easy, man. Save it for the fight," one of them said with a calming voice.

Tanner grabbed Kaine's trainer by the neck, lifting him off his feet with one hand. Kaine's trainer tried to release himself from the boxer's clutch, violently swinging at Tanner's forearm and kicking him in the ribs. Nothing seemed to work to free him from his grip. Another one of Kaine's entourage tried pushing Tanner, but the boxer managed to clutch his neck. He started to squeeze tightly, and in moments, both men were on their knees, grasping at Tanner's hands and noticeably struggling to breathe. Finally, Tanner released his grip, and the two crumbled to the floor, gasping for air.

Tanner spotted Kaine heading towards the exit. He started to race towards his opponent, but his body froze in mid-step, from being tasered by Casino security. He tried to fight through the pain, but he collapsed to the floor.

Tanner lay on the carpet for a long while. He was face down, spread-eagled on the floor in handcuffs. Several security officials were on their knees, quietly talking to the boxer. Aimee watched from a distance as hotel security was unwilling to let anyone near Tanner while they tried to diffuse the situation.

The security staff looked at each other, nodded, and proceeded to lift Tanner to his feet. The young fighter stared at the convention floor to avoid looking into the security guards' eyes as he faked his calmness in an effort to persuade them to remove his handcuffs. He repeated calmly, "I'm all right now."

One of the security staff unlocked his handcuffs, and Tanner took a deep breath. He turned quickly in both directions looking for his sister. He spotted Aimee and pushed towards her. Reporters thrust themselves in front of him, as a flurry of questions ensued.

"What did you think when Kaine insulted you and your sister?"

"Do you have a statement for Kaine's camp regarding this incident?"

Tanner reached Aimee, took her hand, and started parting the crowd of reporters; the siblings headed towards the exit. The media followed relentlessly with their questions.

"Las Vegas experts predict you will be knocked out in the first round. Would you care to comment?"

Tanner moved the last of the reporters from their path and opened the big mahogany door. The young boxer discovered the promoter, Midas, standing on the other side with a dozen hotel security staff. He was smiling, but the security staff stood motionless. They had created a semi-circle just outside the convention door so that no one could pass. The shouts behind Tanner and Aimee became whispers. The promoter placed his hands in the air and asked for silence. Beaming, he looked at Tanner and Aimee, and then turned his eyes to the sea of reporters flocking to his new marketing miracle.

He started, "Yes, these two are quite a story. So many of your questions are still unanswered, and you will have your answers." He paused and then continued, "But not today." Midas then stepped aside and waved Tanner and Aimee through. They rushed past security and towards the casino floor. Sounds of disgruntled shouts and dejected voices filled the room.

Tanner could hear Midas saying, "I know, I know, but we have a lot to discuss regarding the big fight tomorrow; now, please sit back down, and I promise to give you some worthy footage."

Security was stepping towards the door in an apparent attempt to keep everyone in the room.

Tanner and Aimee had turned the corner to the sound of slot machines: *Ding-ding-ding-ding-ding, dong-*

dong-dong-dong-dong, sounds of imaginary coins dropping into slot machine pans could be heard throughout the Casino floor. Expressionless faces pulled at their levers, holding a cigarette, a cocktail, or both, as the two moved through the casino unnoticed. Tanner found the walk through the smoke-filled room a welcomed distraction.

Tanner wanted to be alone; he was filled with rage, but Aimee wanted to discuss what had just happened. They entered his suite and Tanner lowered his head and paced across the hotel room. He couldn't forget what Kaine had said. He cursed, shook his head, and punched his fist into his hand.

Aimee watched him for a while, growing impatient. Finally, she stood up and slapped her right hand into her left palm telling him to stop.

He straightened, put his hands to his hips, and turned to face Aimee.

His sister repeatedly slapped her right hand into her left palm. She then created a fist, raised her thumb, and rubbed it against the top of her open hand; she pushed the fist with the thumb raised at her brother. She was shaking and noticeably upset. She'd just told Tanner to stop blaming himself.

Tanner fell onto the couch, placed his hands on his face, and rubbed his eyes. The young man then dropped his hands and stared at the floor. He started, "Ever since that day, I have never been able to forgive myself." Tanner cried softly.

Aimee sat next to him and placed an arm across his shoulders.

Tanner cried, "I should have never left you at the mall—over what—a stupid disagreement about what to buy dad for his birthday." Tanner still struggled to forgive himself. He'd left her at the mall to find her own ride home nearly twelve years ago. While shopping, she'd met some guy who had charmed her and invited her to dinner, but they had never made it to the restaurant. Instead, the young teenage boy opened the car door and then struck her on the back of her head. He'd placed Aimee in the backseat, driven her out to an old, abandoned country road, and raped her. He had then cut off her tongue so she could never speak about what happened.

That fateful day, Aimee had managed to lay still until the car had cleared her view. She was bleeding profusely from her severed tongue. The young girl stood up, and spitting blood, she'd tried to compose herself. Aimee knew the place—it was the same road that Tanner and his friends used to visit on Friday nights to listen to music, drink beer, and talk. She was several miles from the highway, but there was a lake house less than half a mile to the northwest. It was a place where they rode bikes and jumped off the rope swing into the cool waters of Bucks Lake. She'd found a path, leaned forward to keep from swallowing the blood and staggered to the vacant

cottage. When she'd finally arrived, she'd felt faint from

losing so much blood and struggled to stay on her feet.

She smashed the bay window with one of the softball-

sized decorative rocks that outlined the driveway. Aimee

crawled inside over the broken glass, leaving a trail of

blood and dirt. Desperately, she picked up the house

phone and dialed 911. The injured girl whimpered into the

phone. When the emergency crew arrived, they were

stunned that she was still alive.

The attacker was eventually caught in New

Mexico for attempting another rape. This time, his

fortunes changed as the road was not as private as he

anticipated. He was held at gunpoint by a group of hunters

who spotted what he was doing through the scope of their

gun barrels. He was arrested and later murdered in prison

while serving a life sentence.

Tanner had tried to remove himself from the

tragedy his sister had to bear.

Finally, he'd managed to close his eyes and say, "I can't help it. I promise you that our lives will never be the same after tomorrow—that your time to shine is coming soon."

Aimee surveyed the room and saw a pen and paper on the nightstand. She wrote aggressively. She stopped writing, looked up at him angrily, and then returned to her note. She punched the paper into Tanner's chest. It fell to the floor, and he reached down to pick it up.

Her brother read the note out loud, "Who experienced my tragedy? You? No! Me! I didn't ask you to feel my pain! I do not give you permission to defend me! I will defend myself! How dare you think that my life is a tragedy! I will fulfill my dreams without your help!"

Aimee's fists were clenched.

Tanner held one hand in front of the other and squeezed as if he was grasping a rope and then pointed to himself. He told her again, but this time in sign language, to trust him.

Aimee wiped her tears from her eyes and tried to smile; she shook her head and walked out of the suite.

He waited for her to leave before pacing again between the bedroom and the living room. He visualized beating Kaine mercilessly; he sank deeper into the darkness while he shadowboxed his opponent to defeat. Tanner was in a boxing ring. His body soon started sweating, and the familiar smells of the smoke-filled arena returned. He was standing in his hotel room swinging with great force at his imaginary opponent. Tanner could hear his punches punishing Kaine's face and body. It overwhelmed his senses as the rage blinded him from reality. He was soon interrupted by the ringing of his cell phone. It was his father calling.

3

"Son, I wish you would stop this and come home," Kenny pleaded to Tanner. "I need your help on the farm. It's close to harvest time, and there is so much to do. I had to hire more help. Why don't you and Aimee take the first flight back home?"

Tanner closed his eyes and held his cell phone tightly to his ear. Hearing his father plead for his help turned his stomach. Tanner could only respond with, "Dad . . ."

His father started to raise his voice, "I saw what happened today, son! You need to stop with this uncontrollable anger! It's going to kill you!" His father started to cry, apparently shaken by what had happened at the press conference. "Just stop it! Please stop blaming yourself!"

A long, silent pause ensued.

He then said softly, "I wish your mother was here."

Tanner lowered the cell, took a deep breath, and got off the bed. He rested his knees on the floor, placed his elbows against the mattress, and then dropped his head as if he was praying.

Tanner struggled to tell his father and Aimee why he had put himself through this unimaginable, rigorous routine to reach this moment but soon, he thought assuredly, they would be in a better place. Tanner knew they couldn't care less about any prize money he might earn. All his family wanted was for him to be at peace, find a home in this world, and witness his happiness.

"Dad, I promise you, after tomorrow, I will find a better way."

"I'm not watching the fight," his father replied.

Tanner chuckled; he knew he was lying. "The odds are that I have an eight-to-one chance of winning this fight. So bet the farm on it!"

His father replied sarcastically, "Uh-huh, sure. So, what are the odds of me breaking your nose with a thick switch?" His father sighed. "Okay, son—but promise me, please, that this will be the last time you ever lift your fists in anger. You need to resolve your rage with that beautiful mind of yours, not with violence. Can you promise me this, son?

"As soon as the fight is over, I promise." Tanner took a long breath and said slowly, "I love you, dad."

"I love you, too, son. Give my love to your sister."

Tanner dropped the phone on the hotel bed as his face turned from sadness to anger. He stood up and started pacing, replaying the press conference in his mind. His pace quickened and he clenched his fists, and growled, "I am going to kill, Kaine! How dare he insult my family; I'm going to kill him!"

4

"I'm so proud of you, honey. You were always so loving, but it's time to let your brother go," said Patricia, as she brushed her daughter's hair.

She would occasionally kiss the back of her head between brush strokes.

"I know, mom. He won't forgive himself," Aimee replied softly.

"Yeah, well, he is a grown boy now. He needs to find his way. I love how close the two of you are, but it's time you separate and live a purposeful life. What do you want to do with your life, angel?"

"I want to help battered children. I want to tell them that they are special and powerful and can bring about amazing changes in this world."

Patricia stopped brushing and rested her chin against Aimee's shoulder. "Aw, I love your heart. You are so strong-willed and passionate. I can't wait to witness you sharing and loving these children."

"You are right, mom, it's time we both separated from each other. He has never left my side since I was in the hospital." Aimee lowered her head and cried, "It was his way of saying I'm sorry. I just want him to be happy— to be at peace. He used to love reading books and sharing everything he was learning about this life. He would have been a brilliant scientist!"

Patricia stood up, moved in front of Aimee, and kneeled. She lifted her daughter's head and wiped her eyes. "Angel, I'm here to tell you that as soon as you and your brother take different paths, you will both heal. There will be no more regrets. I promise you."

Aimee woke up with tears rolling down her cheeks. It was the first time she had ever dreamt of her mother. She got out of bed and dressed. She then stopped, pointed at the mirror, and silently mouthed the words, "After this fight, I'm done with this." She lowered her head and closed her eyes as she tried to relax. Kaine was a thug. It made her chest hurt when she thought of her brother being beaten mercilessly in the ring. Aimee shook her head and opened her eyes to erase the thought from her memory. She dropped the brush on the vanity and hurried into the bedroom to grab her gear.

Aimee sat at the edge of the hotel bed and focused on the fight. She reviewed their strategy in her mind. Then, she rechecked the bag to ensure she had all the necessary supplies. Finally, Aimee Childress was ready for the most significant moment of her brother's young life. She marched across the hall and knocked on Tanner's hotel room door.

The door opened quickly. Aimee stepped back and panicked when the smiling face of Midas greeted her. He was wearing a solid, gold-sequined jacket, white slacks, and gold leather boots. His black hair was neatly combed up and slightly back. He must have used a bottle of hair gel to keep it in place.

He called, "There she is," and then laughed.

Aimee tried to smile. He made her nervous. They didn't see characters like Midas in West Texas.

The promoter stepped back and gestured for her to enter. Tanner was sitting on the couch in the living area, reading through legal documents. Two diminutive men wearing black suits holding open briefcases on their laps sat on either side of Tanner. He lowered the papers and looked at his sister.

She was wearing her game face.

He grinned at her and deliberately turned to one of the lawyers, and asked, "What does this paragraph mean?"

The lawyer cleared his throat, and said, "Well, Mr. Childress, in the event you were to incur medical expenses or become deceased as a result of today's fight, you will not hold Midas or any of his business partners liable."

"I see. Does this include being fatally spiked by one of Midas's permanently glued hair follicles," he asked, closing one eye and pointing at the promoter.

Aimee giggled and smiled at Midas.

The colorful promoter laughed so loudly that it echoed throughout the hotel room.

Tanner picked up the pen from the coffee table and signed the contract. He stood up and walked towards Midas, never losing eye contact. He held out his hand and said confidently, "Thank you, Midas, for offering to be my promoter. Let's get through this fight, and I promise you, I will speak to you first before I consider any other offers."

Aimee's eyes widened. Tanner winked at her and looked back at Midas, and said, "I need to get ready—I'm going to kill your champion. By the end of the day, I expect the ten million dollars to be wired into the account I referenced on the contract."

Midas lifted his head and laughed again. He then said in a calming tone, "Good luck, son. You understand this is a 'winner take all' tournament. There is no money for second place."

"Perfect," the young boxer retorted, "I want that mouthy punk to use his own money to pay for his funeral."

Midas's face turned somber, and he looked worried. The promoter waved at his legal team to follow him out of the room. He looked back at Tanner and Aimee for a long moment and then quietly closed the door.

Aimee punched Tanner in the shoulder. She

pointed at Tanner and then at the door—extending her middle and index fingers, she pressed them against the top of her hand.

Tanner nodded, and said, "I know I make him nervous. I want him to be on edge. When I win today, he will make certain we get paid."

Aimee rolled her eyes, shook her head, and let out a helpless laugh.

Tanner's face turned red. He grabbed her shoulders, so she was facing him directly. He leaned forward and said softly, "I will give him a beating he will never forget."

Her stomach turned, and she lost her breath. She needed to be strong one last time for her brother. Aimee clutched her bag and headed towards the door; Tanner understood it was time to go to work.

They silently walked out into the hotel hallway to head out towards the arena; Aimee and Tanner would not communicate again until the bell rang to stop the fight.

5

Tanner and Aimee entered the arena spotlight. The crowd roared while a song with a heavy drumbeat blasted over the loudspeakers. Stadium security attempted to keep them from the outstretched arms of fans who wanted to touch the new boxing sensation. Tanner placed an arm around Aimee's shoulders and motioned for her to keep her head down. They followed the security team until they reached the edge of the ring.

Tanner stepped into the ring. His skin was red from the rage that pumped through his veins. He stood motionless, staring at the champion's entranceway. The music changed to a rap song Kaine had composed himself. Arena lights soon revealed him marching in with his entourage. The crowd chanted, "Kaine! Kaine! Kaine!" They were pumping their fists in the air.

My name is simply Kaine

The one name brawler

Who makes it rain with pain

Here comes the lightning

Ha, fool, don't even try to run

My thunder is frightening

Punching you ignites me

You better pray that I only

Make you pay

With a bloodied face

And hidden scars

With fears, you can't erase

Ha! You, standing against me

Not for long, loser!

All your thoughts

Your plans

Your dreams

Replaced

With only the memory

Of being disgraced!

By the king.

That's right!

Of the ring!

There can't be another.

Here comes the pain!

I am!

I am!

Kaaaaaine!

Tanner's arms were resting on the ring's top rope.

He started to breathe deeper and a little faster.

Kaine's team surrounded him as he pumped both

fists in the air while his fans continued shouting his name.

He was wearing gold-colored trunks and a matching robe.

It was the same color Midas wore at ringside. Tanner

fixed his gaze on the promoter. The colorful man clapped

enthusiastically as his champion entered the ring. Midas

turned to look at Tanner. The promoter was startled to see

the red-headed challenger staring at him. His smile

vanished and his face turned expressionless as Midas

waved awkwardly at the young boxer. The promoter

nervously adjusted his gold-sequined suit, glanced over at

Kaine, and proceeded to sit down.

Tanner looked at Midas for another few moments.

"I don't care if he wants his champion to win," he

whispered, "I'm kicking Kaine's ass, and the prize money

will be in my sister's hands by the end of the night." He

took another deep breath and returned to staring at Kaine.

The champion walked over to the ringside, where

the promoter was sitting, leaned against the ropes, and

shouted, "Midas, watch me beat this hillbilly into retirement."

The promoter chuckled and lowered his head. He must have felt Tanner's gaze because he peered out the corner of his eyes at the young challenger.

Kaine followed Midas's eyes, pointed at Tanner, then punched his fists together. The champion bounced between his trainer and his corner while shadowboxing, stopping intermittently to chuckle.

Tanner assessed his opponent. *He is too relaxed,* Tanner thought, *I need to piss him off to end this fight quickly.*

Aimee stood outside the ring, watching her brother. The young manager started shaking; the moment was too much for her. She decided to sit on the stool reserved for Tanner just outside the ring, and took a drink from his water bottle.

Tanner turned to look at her. She nodded, lifting

the water bottle. Aimee let out a helpless laugh. Her brother tried to speak, but the young fighter was interrupted by a tap on his shoulder. It was the referee as he reached for his gloves and checked them for any foreign objects. Once satisfied, he motioned Tanner to the center of the ring.

Kaine approached the center with his manager. His chest was flexed, and his chin jutted out. He stood waiting for Tanner. The young boxer walked towards Kaine confidently. They continued to stare at each other.

Kaine started to yell, "Come feel my pain, hillbilly!"

Tanner pushed him, which caused Kaine to fall awkwardly into his manager. The referee stepped between the two fighters pressing a hand against each of their chests to separate them.

Kaine was livid. He gathered himself, then threw a violent right cross that missed Tanner, but his elbow struck the referee in the cheek. The referee absorbed the blow as he lowered his body and grabbed Kaine around the waist.

Tanner decided to turn his back and walk casually towards his corner. The excited arena crowd muffled the screams of Kaine's rant. For several minutes, the referee continued to address the champion in his corner. Kaine's entourage was gripped with hysteria. They were pointing at Tanner and shouting at the referee. A few more minutes passed before the referee successfully tempered their anger and they finally nodded in agreement.

Tanner turned to his sister raising a thumb, "It worked! He's mine now!"

The referee walked to Tanner. The left side of the referee's face was beginning to swell and change color from Kaine's blow. The referee stood confidently in front of Tanner, squeezed the young boxer's wrists tightly, and said, "If you pull that stunt again, I will disqualify you. Do you understand?"

Tanner responded with a nod, his face expressionless.

The referee continued, "Okay, we'll forget about the shaking hands bit. The bell will sound as soon as I walk to the center of the ring, and then you both can proceed with beating the hell out of each other."

The referee let go of Tanner's wrists.

Tanner continued to poke at Kaine's temper. He pointed at the boxer, and shouted, "Hey, Kaine! Kaine!"

Tanner moved a glove across his neck.

The crowd responded with a deafening roar. Kaine screamed as he lifted his head towards the arena rooftop.

Tanner noticed saliva seeping from the edges of his lips. The champion paced relentlessly in his corner.

"Perfect," Tanner mused, "now I'll beat him until he's unconscious."

The bell rang, and Kaine ran towards his

challenger. He lunged with his right hand, but Tanner anticipated the punch and moved gracefully to avoid it. Kaine nearly lost his balance but recovered to throw a violent haymaker with his left that missed. Tanner leaned back as Kaine continued his assault. The champion eventually managed to strike Tanner's shoulder, which Tanner had strategically turned to give him the opportunity to counterpunch. The posture meant the left side of Kaine's face was wide open. Tanner hit him with his right with such great force that Kaine stumbled slightly, and his arms fell as he tried to regain his balance, which allowed Tanner to hit with a left hook just above his nose. The champion tried to lift his right arm to protect himself from another left hook, but Tanner crouched and used the force from his lower body to punch Kaine with a devastating right cross that dropped the champion to the canvas.

The crowd was stunned.

The champion managed to get back up on his feet quickly, but he was hurt badly.

The referee held Kaine's arms and counted to eight.

Kaine looked away from the referee and shouted at Tanner, "It's on now! I'm going to whip your country ass!"

Tanner pointed at him with his left hand, placed his right hand on his stomach, crouched, and laughed.

Kaine screamed.

The referee released Kaine. Tanner continued to taunt Kaine, waving him closer with both hands. The champion punched his gloves together and lowering his head, he charged straight into Tanner's abdomen driving the kid to the floor.

The young Texan groaned from the impact. However, he maintained his composure and kept mocking Kaine, laughing as he covered his face from the barrage of punches aimed at his head.

The referee jumped in and rolled Kaine off Tanner. Then, he placed his body between the contestants as the bell rang to finish Round One.

The referee crouched over Kaine, lecturing him about the illegal act of tackling the challenger in the ring. Tanner was the first to get to his feet. He leaned over the referee's shoulder and looked directly at Kaine.

"This is boxing, stupid, not UFC," Tanner said, as he strutted towards his corner.

Kaine jumped to his feet, and yelled, "C'mon! Where are you going, fool? I'm just getting started!"

The referee placed both hands on Kaine and pushed him to his corner, threatening to disqualify him if he didn't follow the rules.

Kaine's team eagerly waited for him to sit down. His manager shouted, "You're getting him champ! You showed him!" The champion had instilled fear in his own crew who were afraid to give him any sound advice.

Scantily dressed, a beautiful woman rubbed his shoulders

while another rubbed a cool, moist towel against his face

as his crew shouted words of encouragement.

"Nice move!"

"You got this, now!"

"Rope a dope, his ass!"

Tanner stood in his corner. He turned and winked

at Aimee, who was sitting on his stool outside the ring and

continued to drink from his water bottle. She let out a

nervous laugh, handed him the water, and he had a quick

drink. He turned to face the champion and leaned his

shoulders against the ropes.

He cupped his boxing gloves around his mouth,

and shouted, "I love the circus show, Kaine! Especially

the clowns!"

Kaine stood and began pushing his staff away. He

picked up his wooden stool and tossed it against the

concrete floor just outside the ring. It bounced a few times, causing his crew to scatter.

Tanner made the gesture of running his thumb across his neck again.

Kaine started towards the center of the ring, but the ref hurried over and reminded him to wait.

The bell rang, and the crowd roared.

Kaine sprinted towards Tanner with his fists clenched.

The champion continued to swing violently with both arms as he chased Tanner around the ring until Kaine's arms began to slump below his chin.

Tanner noticed he was tired. The challenger stepped away from Kaine's reach and quickly turned towards Aimee. She stood, dropped the water bottle, seeing the change in the champion's posture. They had talked about this moment for a long time, and they both knew it was about to arrive. She raised a fist above her head. Tanner knew what that meant; he lowered his body and pushed Kaine back into the ropes. Then, he began hitting him mercilessly, growling as he threw one violent punch after another.

The referee had seen enough, and tried to grab Tanner's arm, but the challenger's elbow struck him on the bridge of his nose. The referee stumbled to the canvas. Tanner continued to hit the champion in the face. He was shouting at Kaine, "I'll show you respect!" He grunted as he landed another brutal punch to his skull—Kaine was bleeding from both eyes.

"What's that? Nothing to say?" Tanner yelled.

Kaine leaned over to keep his balance, but Tanner stood him up with his left arm and pushed him back against the ropes. The challenger lifted his right arm, turned his torso, and screamed as he unleashed all his anger onto Kaine. The vicious right cross struck his temple with a devastating impact that caused a loud popping sound. The gruesome noise shook Tanner from

his rage. He lowered his arms and slowly stepped back,

watching Kaine bounce off the ropes and drop headfirst to

the floor.

The referee, who'd recovered from his fall, pushed

Tanner aside and rushed to the unconscious fighter.

The challenger clutched at the seams of his trunks

while he leaned forward to catch his breath. Tanner

looked down at his gloves as blood dripped onto his shoes

as well as the floor. He slowly walked back towards his

corner. A few muffled cries could be heard from the

startled arena crowd. Medical staff raced to the ring, as

they slowly turned the fighter over on his back—it was

clear that Kaine was not moving.

Tanner looked for his sister, and saw that she was

crying, holding her head in her hands. He tried to speak,

but he was in shock. Aimee sensed her brother

approaching and looked at him angrily. Aimee made a

chopping motion with her left hand against her open palm, pleading for Tanner to stop.

"Aimee, please." He stepped over to her.

Aimee lifted the stool over her head and threw it at her brother. It landed a few inches from his feet. She clutched her stomach as tears filled her face. Her brother stood still. Then, seeing Kaine's blood smeared across Tanner's body, she let out a guttural scream. She covered her mouth with both hands and stepped farther away, and Tanner watched helplessly as Aimee sprinted towards the arena exit. He looked back at Kaine, who was still unconscious. The medical team was applying a defibrillator to his chest.

Midas purposely stepped in front of Tanner to prevent him from watching the medics. The promoter leaned towards him, and said, "Son, you have been paid. You need to get out of here now. There is nothing you can say to fix this disaster. Call me in a few weeks."

Tanner tried to back away from Midas; he wanted to approach the medics.

But instead, Midas grabbed Tanner by the shoulders as he shouted, "Get the hell out of here—now!" The promoter had a desperate look on his face as beads of sweat fell from his temple.

Tanner remained in shock. It took him a moment to understand Midas's pleas. He finally dropped his shoulders and turned back towards his corner. The young Texan peered at the audience. People stood with their hands over their mouths, their horrified looks caused Tanner to lower his head. He wanted to escape. The boxer's gloves were covered in blood. He tried to wipe it off on his white trunks, but only managed to smear more blood onto his clothes. He turned again to face the promoter; he wanted to say something to Midas, but nothing he could say would make sense of what had just happened.

Midas saw he was struggling, and quietly repeated, "You need to leave now, son."

The promoter watched Tanner slowly exit the ring. He then hurried over to Kaine to help the medical team.

Tanner stared at his feet as he walked to the locker room. No one said a word to him, but they continued to stare, mortified by his blood-stained body—a reminder of his vicious rage.

6

Tanner sat alone in his locker room, fumbling to remove his gloves using his teeth. He was trembling and breathing heavily. He removed the laces from his teeth and shouted towards the door, "Can someone help me?" Tanner could not stand up; he was still in shock. He dropped to the floor and placed the boxing gloves over his eyes. "What have I done?" he cried.

A few minutes later, he heard the sound of the locker room door opening, followed by a familiar voice. "Son?"

Tanner lifted himself off the floor. He looked briefly at his father, and then lowered his head. "Dad?" he began to sob, "I'm scared."

His father leaned down and rubbed his head as tears fell from his eyes. "I know, son," he choked, "your anger turned you into an uncontrollable monster. No one is safe around you. Not even yourself." He lifted his son's arm and began removing his gloves.

Tanner continued to look down at the floor.

"It's time we forgive our past. You need to find your purpose in this life." He pulled the bloody gloves from Tanner's hands and found the nearest garbage can. He threw them in the trash. "You won't be needing these anymore."

His father's face changed from somber to stern. "Stand up, son. I need to talk to you."

Tanner stood but continued staring down at the floor.

"Look at me, son."

Tanner raised his head as he struggled to keep from crying.

His father stepped closer and said softly but firmly, "I'm not going to witness this behavior anymore, and neither is Aimee." Kenny paused a moment to let the words sink in. "I love you, son. Aimee loves you. But we can't live with what you've become. You need to find your purpose in life, and you need to let your sister find hers."

Tanner nodded. "I need to go away, huh?" he choked.

His father pulled his son into his arms, as tears filled his face, "Yes, son. For now. Go find Tanner, the man—the beautiful, intelligent man—that I always dreamed you would become."

"Okay," he sobbed, "I will. I love you, dad."

Kenny released his son from his embrace. He

rubbed his son's shoulder, and said, "We need you to come home, but we all need to heal first." Kenny stepped back and looked at his son and then placed his hands on his hips. "You need to clean up. Go back to your room, wait for your sister, and say your goodbyes. I won't tell her about this conversation. You tell her what you need to, and I'll text and let her know that she needs to go to your room in the morning."

They shook hands and smiled.

"See you when I see you, son." His father walked towards the door.

"I love you, dad! I got this!" Tanner shouted,

His father raised a fist above his head as he exited the locker room.

7

This is Trey Winkler with *Channel 5 Sports*. Last night, Las Vegas may have witnessed the most violent display of boxing in modern history. We will be showing you a clip of this fight in a few moments. We must first warn you that viewer discretion is strongly advised, and it is certainly not suitable for children. The first annual United States Boxing League Round Robin Tournament championship between the fighting legend, known only as Kaine, and an unknown amateur boxer named Tanner Childress, turned into tragedy. We will now show the footage. Again, viewer discretion is strongly advised.

Kaine is wearing gold trunks, and his face is covered in

blood. To the referee's credit, he tried to stop the fight, but

he was knocked to the ground after being struck in the

face by Tanner Childress's elbow. Now watch what

happens next. The fighter begins to scream at the helpless

boxer trapped against the ropes. He was beaten and nearly

unconscious, but . . .

A loud knock forced Tanner off the couch. He

opened the door to let Aimee inside. She had her suitcase

and heard a news broadcaster comment:

"That is horrifying. Why do we allow boxing to

continue? The man lost his life, for Christ's sake! That is

not a sport! Trey, what is being done about this?"

Aimee dropped her suitcase, grabbed the remote

from Tanner's hand, and turned off the television. She sat

down on the couch, signaling Tanner to join her. Aimee

shook her head and brought her hands together, and then

touched the tips of her fingers. His sister made a fist with her right hand and slapped it against the palm of her left hand.

"I promise, Aimee. I will never raise my fists in anger again." Tanner lowered his head; Aimee smiled, grabbing her brother's hands. He felt the loving warmth of his sister's touch. It temporarily softened the immense pain emanating from his chest. He looked at his sister for a long time. No words could describe how much he loved her.

Aimee signed to her brother that he needs to stop blaming himself.

"I promise, I swear to you, Aimee. I'm no longer going to live with this guilt. I can't, it's killing me inside." Tanner pulled a bank card from his wallet and handed it to Aimee, and said humbly, "This is for you. The bank account is in your name. I had Midas set it up. The PIN is 1-2-3-4. You might want to change it though; there's ten million dollars in the account."

Aimee's eyes widened; she shook her head back and forth as she dropped the card in Tanner's lap. She stood, folded her arms, and moved away from her brother. The bank card represented something evil, and Aimee refused to take it.

Tanner continued, "I've made up my mind, Aimee, and there's no changing it. You can give all the money away if it makes you feel better or use the money to help dad with the farm."

Aimee signed to her brother, "What will you do now?"

Tanner replied, "What about me?" He looked down, took a deep breath, and replied solemnly, "Aimee, I don't even know who I am. I've harbored your tragedy in every thought since that horrible day and I need to find the real me." Tanner then straightened and slapped his thighs, "I want to go somewhere remote to clear my head and reset my soul—after that, maybe an adventure to find a purposeful life. I need to acclimate myself to people in a loving and healthy way." His jaw tightened as he said softly, "I need to love something other than you and dad. I feel empty inside, I want to fill this emptiness with someone or something special."

He smiled at his sister, and add, "My challenge is to forgive myself, forgive God, and the Universe, for what has happened to you, Kaine, and mom, and build a spiritual relationship with this world. That is what I will do. When I discover that relationship, I will return home."

Aimee held her hand over her heart, truly touched.

Tanner got up, handed her the bank card, and held onto her.

Aimee was relieved. Finally, he could try to put this guilt behind him. She released herself from their embrace; she was beaming. Aimee raised her closed hand to her temple and then extended her index finger towards the ceiling.

"Thank you, Aimee, for understanding. You know how much I truly love you. Don't worry about me. I'll come back home but don't wait for me. It's going to take some time."

Aimee placed the bank card in her wallet. Then, she picked up her suitcase while extending her thumb, index, and pinky finger with her free hand.

Tanner tried to smile, feeling more at peace with his decision. "I love you too. Be safe and don't worry about me. It's time for both of us to find our way."

Aimee nodded and squeezed his arm, then walked out the hotel door.

He watched her exit down the hallway—this was going to be the first time they wouldn't be together since she'd fought for her life in the hospital.

Tanner walked back into his room. He immediately dropped his cell phone into the trash. The former fighter sat down on the couch, turned on the TV,

and changed the channel to a documentary about a crab

fishing boat navigating the Bering Sea's treacherous

waters.

    Maybe that is something I could do, Tanner

thought, *an adventure to the middle of nowhere.*

8

It was late afternoon in Ipiluni Kum'agyak. The harbor was full of commercial crab fishing boats, and Tanner was looking for a job on one of the vessels.

He approached a familiar face—the man was checking his cargo before loading it onto his boat. The captain's head was buried in his clipboard, making notes. The sound of Tanner approaching distracted him and he stopped writing. "Still looking for work?" he chuckled.

"Yeah, for the last two months, none of you guys will give me a chance."

"I respect your diligence, Texan. That's right. You have already earned a nickname around here. We are two days from opening season. Keep walking the harbor. Someone will need you."

Tanner's spirits rose and he said, "Thanks, captain." He walked away and then abruptly stopped, shouted at the captain, and waved, "See you tomorrow!"

The captain laughed and raised his thumb.

Tanner decided to walk up to a nearby cliff to visit his new friend Oscar. Every day, after Tanner finished walking the pier, he went up to the harbor's highest point and talked to Oscar about his day.

After a lengthy climb, Tanner set his backpack on the ground and rested on a long, flat piece of shale. It was only a matter of seconds before Oscar greeted his friend.

"Wuh! Wuh! Wuhwuhwuhwuh wuh," the crazy auk pleaded with him for fresh cut shad. He waddled back and forth, high stepping his tangerine-colored webbed feet, with wings folded behind his back.

Tanner laughed, "Oscar, you lazy, chubby boy. You need to get a job!"

The bird flapped his wings and opened his mouth.

Tanner sat quietly overlooking the harbor filled with fishing boats preparing for the king crab season opening. "I understand, buddy. I wouldn't dive into those cold waters either."

Tanner tossed Oscar a fresh cut of shad.

Oscar continued to parade back and forth. The auk was fixated on the small package of shad Tanner held in his arms.

"I'm frustrated, buddy." He tossed Oscar another piece of shad. The hungry auk gulped his food and started to flap his wings. "Wuh! Wuh! Wuhwuhwuhwuh wuh!"

"Well, thank you for asking, Oscar. I'm frustrated because I can't find work."

The sounds of ocean waves and the crazy auk's

pleas for food forced Tanner to smile. A strong gust of Arctic wind lifted Tanner from his slouch. He breathed in the sea air slowly; it was a nice change from the dust-filled skies of West Texas. Tanner had grown a beard, and his hair now nearly reached his shoulders. He dumped the remaining shad several feet in front of him and Oscar finished eating. The auk started beating his wings and waddling back and forth.

"I don't have any more fish, Oscar!" He held out his palms for the auk to see. It was a ritual they went through every afternoon. Oscar finally understood and flew from the ledge, leaving Tanner alone.

Another Arctic breeze shook the young Texan from his thoughts about his conversations that morning. Tanner leaned back and clutched the rocky surface beneath him. He stretched his legs and then got to his feet. The sun was close to setting, and the evening chill was creeping into the harbor. He slowly descended the rocky ledge until he reached the outskirts of the tiny fishing village, Ipiluni Kum'agyak, which meant "Happy Eagle" in Alutiiq. The smell of freshly cooked fish and the groaning hulls of harbored boats welcomed Ipiluni Kum'agyak every evening. Tanner noticed a bustle of activity underneath the lights of the fish processing plant. Nearly all the village residents worked in the plant. The king crab season, although short-lived, was an integral part of the village's local economy—the fishing crews needed supplies, food, and sometimes lodging and, most importantly, a place to unload their bounty.

Tanner made his way to his regular haven, the Thirsty Eagle, the familiar white stucco building peeling from corrosive salts delivered by the Arctic gusts from the harbor. The tavern functioned as an oasis in the middle of a frozen paradise. A faded mural depicting an eagle with its talons clenched and wings opened covered the bar's front wall. The place was unusually busy today, with fishing crews taking advantage of their last available hours before heading to sea.

No one seemed to notice him as he meandered to a lone seat at the very end of the bar. Loud laughter and conversation filled the smoky room. The Thirsty Eagle was warm and dimly lit. Misty eventually made her way over to Tanner and set a pint of dark ale in front of him.

"Any luck finding a vessel?" the shapely, brown-haired, charismatic bartender asked. She had deep, loving, dark blue eyes that touched the soul of anyone that gazed into them. Tanner found comfort in her company. He leaned over and shook his head.

"Not yet, Misty. I was hoping that . . . "

A short, gray-bearded man wearing a black pea coat and a wool cap leaned between them and shouted in a hoarse voice, "Misty!" His arms opened, and a burst of raspy laughter ensued.

"Hey, AJ! It's been a long time—back for the king

crabs?" Misty slapped and squeezed his shoulder.

AJ retorted sarcastically, "No, no, no—I'm at the
Thirsty Eagle because I miss my dark blue-eyed angel!"

He turned towards Tanner, laughed, and greeted
him with a nod. "Oh lord, another fisherman telling lies!"
Misty's smile broadened as she hurried to retrieve her old
friend a shot of scotch and a pint of beer. "Hey, AJ, I'd
like to introduce you to Tanner," she pointed at the
bearded redhead finishing a long swig of his beer.

Tanner stood and leaned towards the man and
shook his hand.

Misty continued, "Tanner is looking for a job."
The bartender looked at Tanner and winked, "AJ is the
captain of the *Obrien*—one of the oldest and most
respected vessels in the fleet." One of the thirsty patrons
called out to Misty and she excused herself and headed to
the other end of the bar.

The captain leaned against the brass rail and

reached into his pocket for his cigarettes. Tanner slid his

chair towards AJ. The older man grinned, thanked him, sat

down, and lit a smoke.

He started, "So you are looking for work, huh?"

Tanner nodded.

"Any experience?"

"None at all, sir, but I'm young and strong. I know

I could be a big help," Tanner smiled confidently.

AJ finished his shot and took a long drink from his

beer. He picked up his cigarette from the ashtray and

looked at Tanner, and said, "Yeah, well, son, my crew has

been with me for over twenty years. We may not be

young, but we understand what needs to be done and what

not to do. I am a third-generation fisherman, and we have

spent most of our lives fishing the Bering Sea. If you

don't know what you're doing, you can get yourself

killed. Or someone else killed!" He lifted his pint and

finished his beer.

Tanner ordered him and Captain AJ another round.

"Where is home for you?" Tanner asked.

"Seattle! Part of the Lower 48, but my heart always remains with Alaska and the Bering Sea," the captain boasted, as he downed his newly arrived shot and took a long drink. His voice became noticeably louder. "You, where are you from?"

Tanner hesitated and decided to tell him the truth. He replied quickly, "I'm from West Texas."

The captain laughed, "Where?"

"West Texas," Tanner repeated. "The only water in West Texas comes from a muddy hole not big enough to float a canoe."

AJ laughed loudly.

Tanner laughed with him.

AJ held out his pint and smiled; Tanner lifted his drink to return the toast. The captain then chugged the entire pint of beer. Tanner did not want to disappoint him, so he emptied his glass of dark ale. AJ burped loudly and raised two fingers in the air at Misty. He finished his smoke and lit another cigarette.

"Why don't you go home, West Texas?" the old man asked.

Tanner, feeling frustrated, waved at Misty for his tab. Then, he turned to the skinny, rugged-looking, diminutive captain, and replied sternly, "I can't go home."

A loud ringtone was heard throughout the Thirsty Eagle. The bar's phone was wired to the speaker system. Misty picked up the cordless receiver and greeted the caller as an old friend. Her voice grew louder, and she turned towards AJ and pointed. The bartender hurried over to the captain and handed him the phone. She said hurriedly, "It's your brother, Douglas."

AJ's face turned pale. If his brother was phoning, it meant something wasn't right with the *Obrien*.

Misty stood out of respect for her friend in case he

needed help.

AJ took a drag from his cigarette and dropped it in the ashtray. He took off his wool cap, pressed the phone against his ear, and placed his free hand over the other ear to muffle the bar noise. He moved his chin towards his chest and leaned forward and shouted into the phone, "Yeah, Douglas. What happened?"

A long pause ensued.

AJ moved the hand from his ear to his forehead.

Misty had returned to serving drinks but kept a close eye on AJ. She raised her hand towards Tanner to let him know she had not forgotten about his tab.

"I can't believe it!" the captain said dejectedly. He rubbed his forehead and started to groan, "I'll think of something. Just keep loading the bait. I'll be there in a few minutes." AJ placed the phone on the bar top and cursed under his breath. He retrieved his cigarette, took a drag, looked over at Tanner, and then at Misty. He quickly returned his gaze towards Tanner. The captain finished his beer and continued to look at Tanner but said nothing.

Then, finally, he shouted at Misty, "Can you send us two more?"

She hollered, "Sure, AJ. On it right now."

In less than a minute, their drinks arrived. Again, AJ downed his shot and, this time only sipped his beer. He held his cigarette in front of him, and then with a somber expression, he started to talk to Tanner.

"That was my brother. Our deckhand, who has been with us for over twenty years, hurt his back." He took a deep breath. The terrible news had noticeably shaken the captain, but he attempted to continue. AJ took another sip of his beer. Finally, he said quietly, "I'm short one crew member." The older man clenched his teeth and looked at Tanner. He was struggling, and Tanner now realized that AJ was trying to ask him to join his crew. The captain sipped more beer, and Tanner grew impatient.

He blurted, "I'll help you, AJ, if you need me."

The captain sat silently appearing to ponder the decision. He finished his beer, put his wool cap back on, and stood. AJ opened his wallet and reached for a handful of dollars. He waved it in the air and then placed it on the bar.

Misty walked over to AJ and grabbed the phone and the money. "Everything okay?" she asked.

"Not really, Misty. I'm down a crew member and forced to hire a lost cowboy from West Texas." He paused and grimaced at Tanner. "Let me pay for the rookie's drinks too."

Tanner beamed but looked confused; he was not entirely sure if he was actually hired.

AJ looked at his new deckhand and ordered, "I want you at the *Obrien* at 4:00 am sharp."

Tanner jumped and barked, "Yes, sir!"

AJ waved good night as he hurried towards the

exit.

Misty reached beneath the bar and pulled out an old bottle of tequila. She poured the two of them a shot. She held up her glass, and Tanner followed suit. Then, with their drinks raised, the bartender shouted and turned to the other patrons. She started slowly, "There are good ships." Misty repeated loudly two more times, "There are good ships! There are good ships!"

The other fishermen heard Misty, lifted their glasses, and chimed in the toast, ". . . and wood ships, and ships that sail the seas. But the best ships are friendships, and may they always be."

The clinking of glasses reverberated throughout the tavern, but Misty held her drink in front of Tanner and asserted, "We don't go to sea because we're young and strong."

He lost his breath as Misty looked deeply into his eyes.

She smirked, finished her shot of tequila, leaned over, and whispered, "Whatever is eating at you, leave it here." The bartender then slammed the empty shot glass down onto the wooden bar top.

"Misty!" a patron from the other end called.

Tanner watched as she walked away. He started to finish his drink but stopped mid-motion and set the full glass on the counter. "I'll come back for this when I return," he shouted at her.

Tanner hurried for the exit, pausing just outside the front door. Then, looking towards the starlit northern sky, with clenched fists raised, he screamed, "Finally, a new beginning! A new adventure! Thank you, God!"

9

It was a late afternoon, but the frigid Arctic wind cut through Tanner's fishing gear as he continued to chop and grind the crab bait of cod, herring, and squid. He was nearly finished. The stench of rotting fish and the ship's dramatic heave through the Bering Sea's turbulent waters caused Tanner to vomit several times. AJ watched him from the bridge. Tanner showed no signs of fatigue.

Douglas approached the wheelhouse and stood next to his brother—they were identical twins.

He studied AJ and tilted his head towards Tanner,

"That kid can work! He hasn't complained once. He must have thrown up three days' worth of food." Douglas started to laugh.

AJ continued to stare at Tanner. He finally responded, "I wonder what his real story is?" He scratched his scraggly, gray beard, giving Douglas a quizzical look, and said, "Do you know he didn't even ask how much the job paid? This isn't about the money for him."

His brother nodded.

Douglas looked back at Tanner and then interjected sarcastically, "Well, he is good with a knife. Maybe that is part of the story."

Douglas opened his eyes dramatically with a startled expression and then his face soon changed to a big smile. Douglas started to laugh, patted his brother on the back, and then walked out of the bridge. He called to AJ, "He's nearly finished with the bait. I'll help him clean up. See you for dinner."

AJ lit a cigarette and took a long, deliberate drag and exhaled slowly. He continued to watch Tanner cut bait with the same urgent pace he had had all day long. He liked this kid, the captain surmised, and couldn't care less about his backstory.

Tanner's hands were bright red. The freezing temperatures, as well as the long days, made it difficult to make a fist. He looked down at the bait tray; he had one more cod to cut. The muscles in his shoulders ached but the fatigue made him happy. Working on a fishing boat required all his strength and focus. His destructive past was slowly being swept away by the frigid Arctic winds and dropped into the Bering Sea's black waters. He breathed easily with an effortless smile.

A longtime deckhand on the *Obrien*, Ignacio, walked up behind Tanner. He placed a hand on his shoulder and leaned over to inspect his work. "Good—you are almost finished!" he noted.

Ignacio, a tall, lean Ecuadorian was also the brother-in-law of AJ and Douglas, and constantly moved throughout the ship. Ignacio rarely slept; he never seemed to tire and loved being on a fishing boat, which was why the *Obrien* only needed three deckhands to fish for crab. The Ecuadorian sang Spanish love songs over the sounds of ocean waves crashing against the ship's hull or whistled melodies with the seabirds that followed their journey through the North Bering Sea.

Ignacio handed Tanner several warm, dry towels, "Wipe off your hands, *trabajador*, which means 'hard worker.' I will finish for you." Ignacio began to sing.

The warm towels brought a welcome feeling to Tanner's aching hands. Then, a few moments passed, and Douglas approached, and Ignacio stopped singing to address him. "This trabajador needs a hot plate of food!"

AJ's twin smiled at Ignacio and then turned to Tanner, and said, "Have you placed all the bait in the cooler, son?"

Tanner nodded, "Yes, sir, except for this last tray."

Douglas responded cheerfully, "Let's go below to the galley. We'll get dinner started. Have ourselves a couple of pulls of some whiskey; maybe we can get to know more about you."

Tanner replied quietly, "Sounds good, sir."

The young Texan turned to Ignacio, who started singing again, and said, "Thank you, Ignacio."

The Ecuadorian smiled as his voice rose higher as he sang an old Spanish melody.

Tanner and Douglas stepped off the deck and made their way into the galley. The ship was still heaving dramatically, making it difficult for Tanner to walk without clutching a part of the vessel with every step.

Douglas stopped in front of the stove as Tanner walked past the kitchen towards his tiny sleeping quarter. His room had enough space for a small bed with a closet containing two wooden drawers. He hung up his wet jacket and grabbed a towel. He turned on the restroom light. The young Texan looked in the mirror, and washed the traces of vomit stains from his beard and brushed his teeth. He clutched his hands together, lifting his arms above his head, the tension in his shoulders soon released as Tanner lowered his arms. He whispered to himself, "First, find your peace by appreciating and loving the universe that surrounds you. Then, when that love starts to pour from you, fill someone's heart."

He walked out of the bathroom with a confident stride. He entered his cabin, hung up his towel, and returned his toothbrush to the closet drawer. Tanner hurried into the galley, where Ignacio and Douglas were sharing a story and the room was filled with laughter.

Douglas held a spatula that he pointed towards Ignacio while saying excitedly, "Remember what AJ said to that college kid?"

They both paused to look at Tanner. He was holding up well; Ignacio and Douglas smiled approvingly.

Douglas lifted his spatula, and said, "I'm grilling burgers. Should be finished in a few minutes. Make yourself comfortable." He then continued with his story. "Remember, Ig? It was so cold that we couldn't keep the ice from forming on the gunwales. So, there we were in the middle of a blizzard, and that college kid stopped baiting the pods and screamed to high heaven."

Ignacio interrupted, "He says, hey guys, it's snowing outside!" The Ecuadorian slapped his hand on the table and started laughing with Douglas.

The cook then turned towards Tanner to finish his story, "AJ heard that cry from the bridge. So, he got on the mic to make an announcement."

Douglas lost his breath, he couldn't stop laughing. "AJ says, that's not snow, son; it's just a little pollen. Get back to work."

The captain peeked his head into the galley.

He winked at Tanner, and said, "I see my brother is at it again." Then, he looked over at Douglas and said jokingly, "Don't chase him off. We've got work to do."

Douglas quipped, "Where is he going to go? He can't even escape from my farts. You keep checking the weather. We don't want to run into a pollen storm."

They could hear AJ laughing as he returned to the wheelhouse.

Ignacio turned to Tanner, and asked, "You're a long way from home. What brings you here?"

Douglas quieted down to listen to Tanner's story as he returned his attention to making dinner.

Tanner looked at Ignacio and then at AJ's brother. He knew they wanted an answer. The young Texan placed his elbow on the table and rubbed his right hand across his forehead. He struggled for a moment as he decided whether to tell the truth or say anything at all. Tanner stuttered, "I uh . . . " He took a deep breath and sat up, and admitted, "I haven't talked about this with anyone."

Ignacio leaned towards Tanner. The Ecuadorian had a good heart; it was easy for Tanner to trust him.

He dropped his hands to his side, and said, "I have lived with a great amount of guilt. So much guilt that it nearly destroyed me. I certainly damaged the lives of my family. My anger also resulted in the loss of another person's life." Tanner told the story of what happened to his sister, Aimee, and how he'd abandoned her that fateful day. "I was determined to make it right for my sister. Becoming a fighter made sense to me. I was angry and frustrated watching Aimee suffer. It was cathartic for me to hit something all day long. I trained, studied, and boxed with Aimee at my side. I qualified for that international tournament in Las Vegas. Ten million dollars to the winner. That was going to be my gift to her. Then Kaine insulted my family on national television."

Douglas's eyes opened wide. He shouted, "You're the one that killed Kaine in the ring!"

Tanner lowered his head to hide the tears dropping onto the kitchen table.

A shot glass full of whiskey was placed underneath his chin.

Ignacio reached across the table, rubbed his shoulder, and said quietly, "This is where you find peace. The sea is our master, our teacher. You won't have time to think of anything else but to catch crabs and how to survive. You picked the perfect place to start your journey."

10

Errr—the ship's buzzer's piercing sound

interrupted the melody of waves splashing over the

vessel's rail and muffled the cries of seabirds. The

buzzing noise meant the captain was ready to bait the first

crab pots and drop them to the ocean floor. It was almost

dusk, as a burst of cold wind forced Tanner to lean

forward and take a deep breath.

Ignacio patted him on the back, and asked, "Are

you alright, *trabajador*?"

"I'm right where I need to be," Tanner smiled.

Douglas and Ignacio managed to set the first crab pot on the lift. The Bering Sea's starboard splash against the *Obrien* soaked everyone on the deck. Ignacio turned urgently to frantically wave Tanner forward as Douglas unfastened a wall of the metal cage. Tanner dropped his head; with a bait bag held in his right hand, he rushed towards the opening of the pot. The young Texan climbed inside the trap. Turning on his back, Tanner fastened the bait to the metal cage's center. He pulled himself out of the pot to allow Douglas and Ignacio to refasten the opening quickly.

Within seconds, another buzzer rang; the lift was raised, and the pot was dropped into the sea. Without hesitation, with the help of a crane, the crew started to pull another empty crab pot off the ship deck as they placed the next trap onto the lift. Tanner rushed to grab another bait bag while Ignacio and Douglas unfastened the crab trap door. The ship's heaving motion made Tanner drop to one knee. He quickly raised himself off the deck with the bait in one hand. Tanner ran towards the cage as soon as the *Obrien* tilted away from him.

This went on through the night. The crew was covered with bruises from slipping on the deck floor and occasionally smashing hands or feet against the ship's rail, but they persevered. The ship's dramatic heaving motion continued until the last crab pot was dropped into the sea.

Tanner straightened his back and placed his hands on his hips turning towards the rising sun. He closed his eyes as he leaned backward, moving his head from side to side. The popping sounds from stretching his neck startled him but sent a warm, tingling sensation throughout his body. He lifted his arms over his head and inhaled the cool, salty breeze gifted from the North Bering Sea. Tanner slowly focused the orange and lavender horizon capped with a seemingly endless pattern of light low lying, gray-colored, moisture-filled clouds.

AJ interrupted the silence, and said, "Let's keep those soaking for twenty-four hours. Come in and get some food in ya' before the pollen storm hits us this evening."

Douglas and Ignacio could be heard laughing as they exited the deck. Tanner looked up at AJ. The captain was standing by the wheelhouse window. He was smiling widely as he waved for Tanner to come inside. Tanner headed towards the galley with both fists raised above his head and thumbs extended.

Ignacio was pulling pans and singing as Douglas grabbed breakfast ingredients from the refrigerator. Tanner made his way to his room, took off his coat, clutched the door jamb with his hands. His muscles were spent from working tirelessly throughout the night. Tanner's thoughts wandered back to the fight with Kaine. The image of him lying unconscious on the floor and then looking down at the blood dripping from his gloves replayed in his mind. He began to tremble as sweat appeared from his temples. He pleaded quietly, "Please, God, help me."

Tanner attempted to calm down by slowly breathing through his nose while shaking his head from side to side.

Tanner made his way into the bathroom. He sank his head under the cold water, which immediately eased the tension from his body. Soon, a knock at the bathroom door forced Tanner to lift his head; he replied quietly, "Yeah?"

"You alright, son?" It was Douglas.

"I'm good, just cleaning up a little." Tanner pulled the plug from the sink. He washed his hands.

The smell of warm maple syrup with fried bacon from the galley put Tanner at ease. "I'll be out before Ignacio starts his next obnoxious ballad," Tanner attempted to laugh.

Douglas replied enthusiastically, "Okay! He's almost through the chorus! At least I think it's the chorus." He chortled as he walked towards the galley.

Tanner mumbled quietly, "One day at a time. Peace will find its way into your heart." He took a few deep breaths and tried relaxing his face by forcing himself to smile. He walked into the galley. Ignacio was pouring pancake batter onto a scalding hot grill. A loud sizzling sound followed by a tiny plume of smoke filled the room. The Ecuadorian also had a pan of bacon cooking on the other burner. Ignacio waved as he continued to sing.

"*Mi amor* (My love)," he shouted, waving the spatula across his body while staring at the ceiling.

Douglas and Tanner chuckled. Ignacio could hear them, which only fueled his theatrics.

He continued his song, *"Lo siento* (I am sorry). "

He raised his voice even more, *"El mar llama mi nombre* (The sea calls my name)!"

"En el momento en que zarpé (The moment I set

sail)."

AJ walked into the kitchen; he farted loudly,

Prrrrrphhhhhhtt.

Everyone laughed except for Ignacio. The loud

sizzling sound from flipping the bacon quickly tempered

the laughter. He sang the remaining words with a tone of

dramatic despair and sarcasm:

"Con estos locos gringos (With these crazy

Americans).

Todo lo que puedo pensar (All I can think about)

Es lo estupido que fue (Is how stupid I was),

Dejar a casa sin ti (To leave home without you)."

That put a smirk on Ignacio's face. As far as the

crew was concerned, Ignacio had just cursed them. Tanner

understood Spanish; he dropped his head and tried to

muffle his chuckle.

AJ filled the room with his scratchy smoke-filled

voice, and said, "Sorry, amigos. I must have stepped on some crab bait." He lifted his right foot playfully to inspect the bottom of his boot. He then farted even more loudly, *Prlpht.*

Douglas groaned, "Whatever it is, I'm sure you're sitting in it now!"

Everyone laughed hysterically. AJ left the galley and headed for the restroom.

Douglas placed an old tin jug of alcohol on the table. He turned a somber face to Tanner, and said, "Today is always a hard day for me." He poured the moonshine into shot glasses. The young West Texan looked at Douglas's troubled face; he quickly turned to Ignacio. The Ecuadorian nodded in quiet approval.

"I lost my brother on this day." Douglas breathed heavily through his nose, wiping the tears from his eyes. He lifted his shot glass and looked up to the heavens, and said, "To my brother Davey!"

The crew lifted their glasses over their bowed heads.

"The Universe's brightest star navigates the *Obrien* through its deadly waters. Its celestial light shines directly into our hearts. May we never lose our direction and drift to nowhere." Douglas tapped his shot glass to the table and then quickly drank the homemade moonshine and everyone followed.

A warm, stinging sensation forced everyone to pucker their lips and swallow the excess saliva that rapidly formed in their mouths.

Douglas refilled their empty shot glasses.

Captain AJ returned from the restroom. He looked at his twin brother with concern, and said, "Be careful, brother. I know it's Davey's day, but we have a nasty storm coming tomorrow."

Douglas mumbled something that sounded more like disapproval. He drank his shot and poured another.

AJ sat down to a plate of pancakes smothered in maple syrup, bacon, and orange juice. His eyes continued to fixate on his brother.

Douglas turned to Tanner, and asked, "Will you drink to my brother, son?"

AJ slammed his fist on the table, which prompted Douglas to shout at AJ, "Why do we have to work in the middle of a damn snowstorm?" He waved his arms at AJ, and asked, "Huh, AJ? Do we need to lose another soul?"

AJ's face turned bright red. He reached over to the table and squeezed his brother's arm.

Douglas swung wildly and missed. AJ pulled his brother on top of the table. The captain managed to hit his brother in the temple, just missing his right eye before Tanner could separate them. The young Texan had AJ in a bear hug, but the captain continued advancing at Douglas, whom Ignacio pinned against the kitchen table.

AJ screamed, waving his index finger at his

brother, "How dare you blame me for Davey's death! Davey is an Obrien!" He pushed Tanner, and shouted, "Let me go! Damn it, son; you better let me go now!"

Tanner released him. The captain backed up towards the door. "The O'briens are fishermen!" He marched out of the galley. The captain quickly returned and wagged his index finger at Douglas while continuing his tirade, "Our ancestors were fishermen! You are a fisherman, brother!" He paused to catch his breath and said quietly, "He was not the only kin the sea has taken from us. It's the price we pay to take its bounty."

Then, the sound of AJ's footsteps leaving the galley was all that could be heard.

Ignacio released Douglas. He looked at the table and then apologetically at Ignacio.

The Ecuadorian shook his head and said, "It's okay, I'll pick this up."

Douglas poured himself another drink.

Tanner looked at his friends, his heart filled with sorrow. He struggled, "I-I-I-I am sorry for your loss." He grabbed his plate, and added, "I am going to finish this bedside."

Douglas released the shot glass from his clutched hand and pushed it away. Ignacio quickly picked up the glass and placed a fresh plate of food in front of him.

The Ecuadorian looked at Tanner; he tried to smile, and said, "Get some rest, *trabajador*. I will wake you up when it's time to pull the pots."

11

"I made you breakfast, sunshine," Kenny held Aimee's plate while she moved her laptop.

Aimee squeezed her father's tummy and giggled. She signed, "I'm happy you are eating."

"I know—this is the best I've felt since your mother passed. I'm so excited for you and your future, and I know Tanner is in a better place." Kenny smothered butter and pancake syrup over his stack of pancakes and Aimee laughed again.

She signed to her father, "Who are you?"

Her dad laughed with her. "I know, right? You used to always make me eat."

He shoveled another mouthful of pancakes, and asked, "What were you looking at on your laptop?"

Aimee wiped her hands on her napkin, reached for her computer, and turned it to face her father.

Kenny read the website's title: *Online Courses for Child Psychology Degrees.*

He set his fork down on his plate and leaned back in his chair, and said, "That's outstanding, Aimee! I couldn't be happier! Do you need help with tuition?"

Aimee flashed the plastic debit card Tanner had given her after the boxing match in Las Vegas.

"Okay, good. I know you can handle your business. A child psychologist, eh? I think that's a perfect choice."

Kenny continued to eat his pancakes.

Aimee reached over and grabbed his forearm to

get her father's attention. She signed to her father, "I need to talk with you."

Kenny took the last bite of food, looked at her cautiously, and then moved his plate away from him, and asked, "What about?"

She signed, "Please go to counseling."

Kenny straightened in his chair and cleared his throat, placed his open palms together and pressed them against his lips while staring out the dining room window at the peach orchard.

A few moments passed. Her father turned to her, and said, "All I ever needed in my life was your mother, you, and your brother. Every morning I'd jump out of bed filled with happiness."

He leaned back in his chair and then rested his hands on his head. Kenny looked out of the dining room window. He paused and then continued, "Your mother and I built this place. Every piece of wood, every nail, every tree and flower we touched with our hands. To this day, she still takes my breath away. I'm always at a loss for words when I think of her impact on my life." He closed his eyes. There was silence in the room for several minutes. Then, finally, he stood, reached for the laptop, and turned the screen to face Aimee. He then cleared the breakfast plates and carried them to the kitchen.

Aimee sat still listening to her father as he washed the dishes—a plate dropped on the floor. He turned off the sink faucet and whispered, "I love you, Patricia. The reason I don't want to go to counseling is I don't want to stop loving you. I can never replace you, my love, but maybe it's time to make a friend."

Kenny walked back into the dining room, and said softly to his daughter, "Find me a counselor. I will go, honey."

12

Patricia, Tanner's mother, played an old gospel song on the guitar to her children on a chilly autumn night. She had long, wavy, auburn hair and wore a homemade, yellow dress with a floral print, as she tapped her foot against the old wooden floor. Tanner's dad entered playing the clarinet. A familiar melody filled the small farmhouse, as it traveled out the front screen door and into the orchards. The smell of peaches filled the living room. They had finished canning, cooking, and drying their bountiful harvest. In her pink pajamas, little

Aimee danced in the middle of the room. Patricia's eyes

fixed on Tanner; she was singing to her son's heart.

Aimee started to laugh with joy as she tried to sing along

with her mother. Soon, Kenny's voice joined the melody.

Aimee and Kenny then sat down on the couch next to

Patricia, as they all sang to Tanner.

I feel your love; its power opens my

eyes.

Now, I see you,

Its greatness grows inside.

Now I hear you,

God calls your spirit,

Closer to your new home.

His dad set the clarinet on the coffee table and

opened his arms for Aimee to sit in his lap as his mother

picked at the guitar.

She continued with the melody:

I love you son.

Your restless heart will soon find her.

Tanner felt his mother's love. Its warmth filled the empty crevices inside his body. He began to hum the tune.

As she lowered her head, her hair nearly covered her face. Tanner could see a tear fall to her cheeks.

Tanner uttered, "Mom, I miss you! I remember your love!

She continued to play the guitar.

Tanner repeated her words, "Your restless heart will soon find her," and was overcome by a revelation, "Oh God, mom, I will find her! She must be someone special!"

Patricia stopped playing the guitar and her face beamed with joy. "Son, release the thoughts from your past. Listen to the messages from the Universe; they will guide you to her. She is your pathway for returning home."

Tanner opened his eyes; he was no longer in the

living room with his family but instead standing in the boxing ring with blood dripping from his gloves. This time the arena was empty. He felt a great calmness. Tanner pulled the gloves from his hands and threw them onto the canvas floor. His shoulders dropped, he took a deep breath, and then quietly replied, "Thank you, mom."

Tanner was awakened by Ignacio. The stream of tears falling from the former boxing champion's eyes startled the Ecuadorian. Tanner quickly covered his face with his hands to hide his tears.

Ignacio stepped back and said quietly, "Let's go, *trabajador,* it's time to touch the restless heart of the Bering Sea."

Tanner jumped out of bed; he quickly dressed while singing his mother's song.

Ignacio shouted from the galley, "It's snowing, *trabajador!* Dress warm!"

He didn't have time to process his dream, but felt a

warm, tingling sensation throughout his body. He'd had the same feeling when his mother was still alive, and the farm was bountiful and thriving.

Tanner made his way into the galley. A bowl of large chocolate candy bars had been left on the table for the crew. He quickly opened the wrapper of one and devoured the treat barely chewing before swallowing. He then opened another one and placed it in his mouth as he hurried towards the deck.

The young man was greeted by a frigid gust of wind, which made him double over. The candy bar dropped from his mouth. Tanner clenched his fists; he tried taking a few long breaths. The deck was sprinkled with ice and snow. The *Obrien* rocked port to starboard slowly as AJ navigated the vessel perpendicular to the Bering Sea waves—it was nearly dusk.

Douglas, wearing his bright orange winter gear, was wiping down the crane's controls. His hood covered his head, protecting his face. Ignacio stood next to a mobile cart fastened against the starboard rail. He whistled loudly to Tanner and waved for him to approach.

Tanner took a step towards him then fell onto the deck. Ignacio whistled again. The young man stood slowly, trying to keep his balance. The Ecuadorian held his hand out, motioning for Tanner to stop as the ship returned to center. Tanner shortened his stride as he quickly made his way and joined him.

Ignacio was excited, and said, "Look *trabajador!*"

He pointed towards the ship's stern. A large stoic-looking bird speckled with white and brown feathers stared at the crew. Then, it bowed at them, turned its talons towards the sea, and flew off with a scream.

Ignacio reached for Tanner's shoulder and shook him, "Do you know the importance of the sea hawk?"

Tanner shook his head no in reply.

"When the sea hawk appears in a place where it is

nearly impossible for them to travel, it is believed the bird is delivering you a message. They bring their medicine from the Great Spirit or God. That, my friend, was your hawk—he brings your medicine!" Ignacio slapped him on the back joyfully.

A smile rested on Tanner's face; meeting this Ecuadorian was no coincidence, he thought.

"Okay *trabajador!*" Ignacio banged his hand against the cart. "After I hook the rigging line and fasten it to the pulley, Douglas will bring up the cage, and it will rest inside the rail. I'll need you to wheel this over to us so we can unload the crab from the cage into the cart. As soon as the cage is empty, return the cart here," he pointed.

He then lifted a ruler that had a caliper on each end, and said, "Then, drop the crab onto this green-colored slide if the crab's shell is bigger than the width of this gauge and has a T-shape for a tail. If the tail looks like an apron or the width of the body fits between the gauge's

calipers, then toss them on the red slide. Understood,

trabajador? T-shaped tails are males. The red slide returns

the babies and females to the sea. The green slide goes to

a tank underneath the deck."

Tanner nodded and raised his voice, "Got it!"

He tried to move the cart, but it would not budge,

so he looked at Ignacio quizzically.

Ignacio leaned over pointing to two hooks that

kept the carriage from careening across the deck, and

explained, "You fasten and unfasten here."

A loud buzzer sounded as AJ signaled the crew

that they were approaching the first buoy. Ignacio turned

and rushed to the portside rail next to Douglas. He

grabbed a large metal treble hook as Douglas pointed

towards the buoy. The Ecuadorian nodded. Turning

sideways, he placed his left foot in front of the other while

twisting his upper body behind him. He crouched down on

his knees slightly and straightened his throwing arm.

Tanner watched Ignacio toss the hook directly onto the

rigging line with great precision. In a few moments, the

buoy was onboard, and the rope was wrapped onto the

crane's pulley.

Waiting for the first crab pot to be lifted off the

seafloor was stressful for the captain and his crew. Only

the sound of waves crashing against the *Obrien* could be

heard. The deck was quiet as prayers were given to God

and the sea. Tanner lowered his head, tucking his mouth

under his jacket to breathe warm air against his skin, as he

held onto the cart. A few moments later, there was scream

of joy from the ship's speakers.

The pot was filled from top to bottom. The cage

was set on a table against the ship's rail as Tanner moved

the cart into position. Douglas and Ignacio released the

cage latches while Tanner rushed to unload the trap's

catch into the basket. Douglas's head was hidden

underneath his cloak but Tanner could make out a somber expression on his straightened lips. Ignacio watched Tanner closely as he returned the cart to the processing area.

The West Texan grabbed the gauge to start measuring and separating the bounty. Ignacio hurried over to help as Douglas stood quietly by the crane, staring at the sea. Normally, AJ would have confronted his brother for not helping with the sorting, but the captain left him alone. Douglas was suffering the loss of Davey.

The snowfall thickened, and the conditions worsened as the night continued. Ignacio started splitting his time, sorting the crabs, and clearing the excess snow from the deck. The crab pots were full, and the crew's spirits were high, except for Douglas. They worked flawlessly, every throw from Ignacio was perfect, every cage was full of crab, and the *Obrien* had nearly reached their limit.

Tanner was sorting crabs when Ignacio approached him—the Ecuadorian possessed limitless energy.

He said enthusiastically, "We have six more pots to go, *trabajador!* I think we will meet our quota after the first run! Can you believe it?"

Tanner smiled; his eyes never left the carriage. His nose was bright red, and his lips were chapped from the cold. The frigid wind constantly reminded him to keep moving and maintain his focus. At some point, his shift would be over. He finished sorting the cart while Ignacio returned to sweeping the deck.

A buzzing sound soon filled the night, and Ignacio returned to the portside. Douglas pointed to the buoy, but the Ecuadorian put his hands in the air indicating that he could not see it. Douglas became animated and kept pointing to the location of the buoy. Ignacio was nervously looking but was unsuccessful in locating the rigging line. Tanner joined them to see if he could help Ignacio find his target.

Douglas leaned over the rail frantically pointing to the buoy, as he yelled, "Over there!"

At that moment, a wave crashed against the *Obrien*. Douglas lost his footing and his grip and was suddenly thrown into the Bering Sea.

Tanner could see him struggling for air as he tried to keep his head above water. Without hesitation, Tanner dove into the water directly at him. The young Texan landed about ten feet from Douglas. He could see the old fisherman was continuing to struggle for air. Tanner's heart raced as he forced himself to not lose sight of Douglas despite the burning sensation of the icy saltwater splashing into his eyes. Tanner lumbered slowly to reach Douglas. The high sea waves made it nearly impossible for him to keep his head above water. Tanner's vision blurred, and he felt disoriented. The two only had a few more minutes to be rescued or die of hypothermia.

Tanner started shouting, "Douglas! Douglas! Douglas!"

Douglas appeared to be in shock. He was not responding to Tanner's calls. Tanner lunged at the man but failed to grasp him. He then dropped his head underwater, kicked his legs while stroking his arms. The Texan finally grabbed hold of Douglas's lifejacket and quickly pulled him to his side. He turned to face the boat and waved his hand above his head. Ignacio promptly tossed the hook towards Tanner, which landed a foot behind him. Tanner flailed his arm at the safety line until he felt it touch the back of his hand. He caught the hook and held onto Douglas.

Above, Ignacio rushed over to the crane and began pulling the two of them out of the sea. AJ, watching from the helm, immediately placed the vessel on autopilot as soon as he saw they were being lifted onto the ship's deck.

Tanner was breathing heavily still holding onto Douglas tightly. He was dizzy and nauseous. Ignacio reached over the rail, wrapped his arms around Douglas, and pulled them onto the deck. Tanner released his grip, which caused him to fall abruptly to the floor. He turned to look at Douglas; the cloud of air escaping his lips assured Tanner he was alive. Ignacio and AJ lifted the old fisherman off the deck and carried him inside.

Tanner's breathing slowed and his body began to shiver. He tried to get up, but he was having trouble maintaining his balance. Soon, Ignacio stood him up, placed an arm around his shoulders, and slowly walked him out of the Bering's frigid air.

Douglas was lying on the galley floor. AJ was quickly stripping the clothes off his brother. Then, the captain heard the galley door open. He shouted, "Ignacio, help me carry Douglas to bed!"

Ignacio laid Tanner down next to Douglas and

glanced at Tanner. The West Texan raised his thumb to signal that he was okay. He closed his eyes and concentrated on his breathing, trembling in his wet clothes.

Ignacio and AJ picked up Douglas and carried him to his quarters. They hurriedly stripped the remaining clothes from his body and wrapped him in blankets.

AJ and Ignacio returned for Tanner, got him to his feet, and marched him to his bedroom and repeated what they'd just done for Douglas. Ignacio called to Tanner, and said, "We need to tend to Douglas."

Tanner moved his head slowly and closed his eyes.

AJ went to the kitchen and started warming up the heating pads. He wrapped them in towels and rushed into Douglas's room. His brother had stopped breathing.

AJ cried out, "He's not breathing!"

Ignacio shouted at AJ, "AJ, get out of the way—move!"

Tanner heard the desperation in their voices.

AJ was in shock. Ignacio grabbed AJ by the shoulders and tossed him away from the bed, then Ignacio began performing CPR. He breathed air into his mouth and pressed his hands against Douglas's chest.

There was no response.

Ignacio shouted, "Douglas! Wake up!"

He continued with CPR.

There was still no response.

Ignacio turned aggressive, and shouted, "You are not leaving now!" He forced more air down his mouth and grunted as he put all his strength into compressing Douglas's chest.

Suddenly, Douglas wheezed as he inhaled air and started coughing up seawater.

Ignacio shouted at AJ, and said, "I need a towel."

The Ecuadorian wiped Douglas's mouth clean.

He gently slapped Douglas on the cheek, and said,

"Wake up, Douglas!"

Douglas continued to wheeze. Ignacio lifted his torso off the bed and slapped his back. Soon, his breathing started to slow, and he opened his eyes briefly, blinking a few times. That was enough for Ignacio. AJ grabbed a few more pillows to elevate his head. They placed a heating pad on his chest. AJ sat at the edge of the bed while Ignacio returned to Tanner's room.

Tanner's eyes were closed, and his breathing had stabilized. He was still shivering. Ignacio placed a heating pad on his chest, put a wool skullcap on his head, and then went to grab more blankets.

Ignacio warmed a glass of brandy and administered several shots to Douglas. The Ecuadorian sat quietly at the edge of Douglas's bed with AJ.

Finally, Ignacio turned to AJ, and said, "I will watch your brother and check on Tanner."

AJ took off his skullcap and rubbed his gray hair.

He looked down as he attempted to find the words to communicate with Ignacio.

Ignacio did not hesitate, and spoke up, "I will not watch another family member die in the Bering Sea! I'm finished, and if you have any compassion left in your soul, you will retire with me." Ignacio got up off the bed and went into the kitchen to heat chicken broth for Tanner and AJ.

The captain remained by his brother's side and mumbled to himself.

13

Tanner remained in bed for the next couple of days. Occasionally, Ignacio entered his room, adjusted his blankets, and forced him to drink a cup of warm chicken broth.

The captain and the Ecuadorian had spent the last two days checking on their rescued crew. The *Obrien* was now heading for the port to unload its bounty.

Tanner groaned, trying to lift his upper body. He could smell maple syrup and bacon coming from the galley. "It must be morning," he thought, as he ran his hands through his hair, scratched his beard, and then stretched his arms.

The excess mucus from his nose made it to his throat, causing Tanner to cough violently. He quickly put on his warmest gear and stepped out into the hallway and headed to the galley.

Ignacio was standing over the stove and held a spatula over his head as he shouted, *"Trabajador!* You are awake!"

AJ was sitting at the table drinking coffee. The captain looked tired, but his spirits seemed to be high. He smiled softly, and said, "Good morning, Tanner."

Tanner's voice was hoarse as he responded, "Hey, good morning, I'll be right back." He sniffled, and added, "I'm going to wash up."

Tanner gingerly made his way to the bathroom. He started a hot shower, and soon, his head was buried underneath the hot water. He drifted back to the moment when he'd grabbed Douglas from the Bering Sea, and felt weak from the weight of the memory. He held onto the shower rail to keep from losing his balance as he breathed heavily through his mouth. The young man tried to clear the mucus from his nostrils unsuccessfully. He exited the shower and leaned against the sink. He gazed into the mirror—his face was swollen and pale. He rubbed his fingers through his thick and unkempt beard. He mumbled, "I don't even recognize myself. It's as if I am staring at a stranger."

He left the bathroom and made his way into the galley. Ignacio was singing while AJ sat quietly, still sipping his warm coffee. The smell of bacon sparked Tanner's appetite. The captain stood, patted Tanner on the back, and retrieved a cup of hot coffee for the kid.

He returned to the kitchen table. AJ started, "My brother and I cannot find the words to thank you. Douglas is actually at the helm, guiding us back to port." His words carried a solemn emotional tone. AJ continued, "The three of us have decided to sell the ship." AJ and Ignacio made eye contact as they both nodded in agreement.

The captain turned to Tanner. Then his face lit up, and his smile widened and he said excitedly, "We are also going to pay you a fourth of the gross share of the revenues, not the net but the gross. We calculate that to be three hundred thousand dollars." AJ took a sip of his coffee. He extended his arms to his sides and asked rhetorically, "How can I put a price tag on saving my brother's life?"

AJ then reached into his pocket and pulled out a bankroll wrapped with a rubber band with a check written for two hundred and ninety-five thousand dollars, which he pushed towards Tanner. The captain said, "You may have trouble getting funds immediately because of the size of the check, so I made sure you have some cash for travel."

Tanner's jaw dropped as he shook his head in disbelief. Ignacio placed a plate of pancakes, bacon, and eggs in front of Tanner. He turned to thank the Ecuadorian, but was interrupted.

Ignacio reached into his pocket and dropped a set of car keys on the table.

Tanner was overcome, "What's this, Ignacio?"

Ignacio responded, "That, *trabajador,* is the vessel that will navigate you through your next journey!" He then handed Tanner a business card with an address. "Call that number when you land in Seattle. My brother will take you to where the car is parked. We will be staying at port to prepare the *Obrien* for sale. Cruise down the oceanside roads, head east, or drive in a circle until you find a place you can call home. Return it once you are settled." He placed his hand on Tanner's shoulder, squeezed it, and said, "Maybe you can shave that mess you call a beard."

He raised his voice dramatically and waved his hands above his head, and said, "A gesture to the Universe that you wish to start anew!" Then Ignacio stepped back and returned to cooking breakfast. He started to sing joyfully.

Tanner was shaken. "I don't know what to say. It seems like I have been fighting my whole life. When my mother died, I searched every book to find answers. When my sister suffered her tragedy, I questioned the pureness of my heart. Did I somehow anger God? I was convinced a great evil was destroying my family. I woke up angry every single day. After what happened in the boxing ring, I realized that my anger was also destroying everything around me. You may not be aware of this, but you have already paid me. The painful memories have mostly subsided, and now I'm ready to live a purposeful life."

The Ecuadorian stopped singing, his eyes saddened by Tanner's words.

Tanner smiled at him, and said, "Don't be sad, *mi amigo, encontré mi propósito* (*I found my purpose*). My mind is no longer consumed with guilt. When I left Las Vegas after burning every bridge I stepped on, I told my sister I had to connect with the Universe. I needed to be able to appreciate not only people but all the wonders of our world. I wanted to smile at the smell of a morning cup of coffee or watch the setting sun and be reminded of the magnitude of our Universe. Here on the deck of the *Obrien*, the cool Arctic breeze has touched every part of my body; I've felt humbled by its force. I'd lost focus of God's creations and now I feel connected again—the same way I use to feel connected when spring arrived on the farm, or a horse gave birth to a new foal. And Ignacio, your selfless acts of kindness to serve others are testimony to what kind of man I want to be. Clearly, the love in your heart overflows, which allows you to effortlessly share your love. That is what I've learned from this experience, and I can't wait to be like you, Ignacio."

Ignacio beamed, "Well, God placed you in front of us, *trabajador*. You were meant to find us, and we were meant to find you." He set a hot plate of food in front of the captain.

"I agree, Ignacio. My mother was in my dreams the other day. She said to listen to the messages from the Universe; that they will guide me to the woman who will lead me home. So, I think I'll get in that car of yours, Ignacio, and stop in towns across the West Coast. I will meet and visit with people, share food and experiences, and keep an eye out for the next message from the Universe."

14

"Welcome to our Widow Support Group, Kenny."

A beautiful, middle-aged, strawberry blonde woman with big, green eyes smiled at the newest arrival in their group. Her name was Stacey.

Kenny's nostrils flared. He could feel Stacey's charm tickle his heart. He tried to speak but only managed to cough.

Stacey reached into her purse and pulled out a small water bottle. She handed it to Kenny.

He cleared his throat and struggled to say, "Thank

you."

Stacey looked at Kenny again and smiled softly, then turned her attention to someone else in the circle.

"Sheila, how are you progressing with your dance club?"

Kenny couldn't take her eyes off Stacey. Sheila was talking to the group, but nothing registered with Kenny. He kept watching Stacey. Occasionally, she'd turn and look at Kenny and smile. Kenny remained expressionless. He felt enamored by her.

"Kenny?"

Kenny didn't respond. He was in her trance.

"Kenny?"

He still said nothing.

The woman sitting next to him bumped his shoulder and giggled, pointing towards Stacey.

"Oh, yes, Stacey, what is it?"

"Tell us about your wife."

"My wife," Kenny sat up in his chair and rubbed his hands against his pants and spoke. "Well, if you believe in soul mates, Patricia was mine. We did everything together and we were happy with that. I understand relationships are different, and that's okay, but we wanted to be together. We planned together, worked the farm together, built our house together, and loved our children with every fabric of our being. It was a rare combination of understanding, intimacy, love, devotion, and sacrifice. I would do anything for her. As the years passed, we didn't even need to speak to understand what we needed from each other, and we were happy to oblige. Not a day goes by when she doesn't still take my breath away."

"That is beautiful," a brunette with spiral curls and a white polka-dotted dress said.

Kenny purposely avoided Stacey while sharing his feelings. When he did look at her, he noticed she was blushing slightly.

"Well, errrm . . . I agree that was beautifully said," she choked.

"How long ago did she pass and what steps have you taken to help you get past your grief?"

"I lost Patricia over fifteen years ago. My daughter has been begging me to seek counseling for years. If it wasn't for her and my son, I probably would have starved to death."

Stacey's eyes widened.

The woman that had bumped Kenny's shoulder laughed loudly, and said, "There is not a single person here who hasn't lost their spouse within the last six months."

Kenny dropped his head and chuckled. He glanced over at Stacey, his heart was fluttering. "I never wanted to heal from loving her, but thanks to my daughter, I now understand that it wasn't about that."

Stacey replied, "Then what was keeping you from seeking counseling?"

"I wasn't ready to say goodbye."

Stacey stood from her chair and turned her back to the group; she could be heard sniffling.

"Please, I need to cancel this week's session . . . please," she pleaded.

The group understood. They picked up their things and quietly made their way to the door.

Kenny stood up; he wanted to say something to her. "I'm sorry, Stacey, I didn't mean to upset you."

Stacey turned around. She looked towards the door to make sure no one else was in the room.

"Will you have coffee with me? I want to talk with you."

Kenny's concerned look softened, and he replied, "I would love to. Where and when?"

15

Several months had passed since Tanner had said goodbye to the *Obrien* and its crew. He'd made his way South along the Pacific Northwest coastline, frequently stopping to visit with the local town folk. Tanner would often remain for several days or sometimes nearly a week, sharing food and drink with people that crossed his path during his journey.

Tanner was on the phone with his father.

"What have you been doing, son?" Kenny asked.

Tanner laughed, "Dad, would you believe

swimming in the Bering Sea?"

His father exhaled, "What? Never mind, I don't want to know."

Tanner shared, "Dad, you're an amazing father. I truly love and respect you. But please trust me when I tell you I'm in a good place. I'm no longer carrying all that anger you used to worry about."

He replied joyfully, "Aw, that's wonderful. Your sister is doing well, too! She is working on the farm, and the money you gave her has changed both of our lives. Thank you, son. We plan on keeping most of it for you when you return home."

Tanner shouted into the phone, "No! Keep it! I don't want a penny of that money! Dad, please," Tanner pleaded, "That money reminds me of the accident in the ring. I can't live with the guilt."

His father seemed to understand and responded in a soothing tone, "Okay, son, Aimee and I will figure out what to do with the money. Where are you now?"

"I'm driving down the Oregon coast in an old Dodge Challenger. I'm forty miles from the California border," Tanner laughed.

"Okay, I'll stop worrying about you. I love you and we miss you. I have your new cell number. I'll call in case of an emergency; otherwise, I'll wait for you to reach out to us."

"Bye, dad, tell Aimee I love her," Tanner ended the call. He stepped on the gas and continued down the scenic coastal highway. He fiddled with the radio for a moment but was unable to find a signal. He sat back in his seat and let up on the throttle as he approached the top of a hill. When he reached the peak, he was greeted by Giant Sequoia Redwood trees as far as the eye could see. Tanner gasped and pulled over to the side of the road. It was about seventy degrees and partly cloudy. A stream of the sun's rays created a mosaic pattern of light with shadows across the Redwood forest. "Only nature could design such beautiful art," Tanner murmured. The majesty of the moment compelled him to take a photo. His thoughts were interrupted by the sound of a large raptor—he couldn't see it in the sky, but he could hear its cry. The air smelled crisp and clean, as the fall scent of forest fauna filled his nose. *This place is magical,* he thought. He returned to his vehicle and lowered all the windows. The loud Hemi engine echoed through the forest when he started the car and pulled back out onto the road.

Later, he approached a roadway sign occupied by a perched sea hawk licking one of its talons. The marker read: *"Whisper—3 Miles."* The sea hawk reminded Tanner of the one that had greeted the *Obrien* crew on the Bering Sea. Ignacio had been convinced the bird was a messenger. He looked at the raptor in his rearview mirror until it was out of sight.

He commented, "Whisper, Oregon. Maybe this

will be my new home."

Tanner veered off the coastal freeway and entered the sleepy little town of Whisper. It was the middle of the afternoon, and the downtown area was sparse. Tanner assumed most people were probably working at a lumber mill or just returning from fishing boats. A park with a small lake occupied the center of the village. An older man wearing a hooded, navy blue rain jacket with long, wavy, gray hair sat on a weather-beaten park bench. He was feeding a small flock of pigeons.

Tanner decided to stop and talk to the man. "Maybe he can tell me a little about this town," he whispered.

The sound of Tanner closing the car door caused the old man to turn, and he smiled and waved. Tanner returned his smile and quickened his pace as he approached.

The old man slid towards the end of the bench,

slapped his hand against its seat and said, "Sit down." The pigeons, startled momentarily, flapped their wings as they retreated a few feet from the visitor. The older man threw some seeds that landed close to Tanner, and the flock quickly moved in his direction.

"My name is Elmer," the man said as he reached out his hand. He offered a gentle smile.

"Pleasure to meet you, Elmer; my name is Tanner," he said as he shook Elmer's hand and continued, "I don't think I've ever met an Elmer before."

Elmer laughed, "And you won't. It's an old Scottish name, it meant "noble and famous" long ago, but I'm happy to report that I am neither." He handed Tanner the bag of birdseed, and suggested, "Why don't you feed my friends?"

Tanner grabbed a handful of seeds and tossed them towards the pigeons. Then, he placed some seeds on his shoes and in front of his feet. Soon, the pigeons surrounded him. Tanner leaned over and admired the birds feeding off his shoes.

Elmer watched Tanner for a moment. He could tell by the distant expression on his face that he was searching for answers.

Finally, the old man interrupted, "Many centuries ago, people thought pigeons were an extension of God's divinity. It was believed they had the power to transform us to be more caring and more loving."

"Well, I could use more pigeons in my life," Tanner admitted. He dropped another handful of seeds for the pigeons.

The older man straightened up and looked at Tanner—a white glow emanated from his eyes as if something greater was speaking through him. "I remember the day I met my Sophie. It was during the war. Millions of people were being slaughtered and enslaved. It was a world of suffering and despair," his voice quavered.

His eyes moistened as he fought off the tears. "How can you find answers in a world full of hate and destruction?" Elmer ran his hands through his thick, wavy, gray hair and his jaw tightened.

After a long pause, he continued, "Well, I was in a radio factory in Utah. My military duties were to make sure naval factories were meeting production. It was a stressful job. At that time, the outcome of the war was not certain. Our men were fighting and dying overseas. Our women worked tirelessly manufacturing, building, and assembling equipment; these very women were also losing their husbands to that senseless war. When I met Sophie, I woke up that morning feeling empty inside. My stomach was aching, and I had no appetite, and I could barely breathe. The war was killing me from the inside."

Elmer stopped and briefly looked at Tanner. The young Texan was hanging onto every word Elmer spoke.

The old man folded his arms, and continued, "I did

my customary walk through the factory, but this time I ignored its sounds. The factory manager followed me through the rows of assembly lines as he recited production numbers and delivery deadlines. I didn't listen to a word of it. I finally said to him: 'What is the point?' This startled the plant manager, and he stammered several times saying, 'B-b-b-but Sir . . .'"

Elmer became more animated, his voice got louder as he raised his hands in the air, "I shouted at him, "Forget it!" I turned quickly to walk away, and as I did, I bumped into this beautiful young angel, who was late in getting to her workstation. As I discovered later, Sophie was never late for work. We crashed into each other and instinctively held out our arms to keep each other from falling. As I held her, my insides filled with warmth. I felt at peace. I had this big smile. She giggled loudly; Sophie understood what I was feeling."

The old man stopped and turned away for just a

moment but returned his gaze. "I think it's time for you to

slow down and find your Sophie."

Tanner tilted his head to the side, blushed slightly,

and lowered his eyes.

"I've met a lot of people on my journey, son.

Granted, not so many in Whisper, Oregon," Elmer

chuckled. "Trust me, Tanner, park that hot rod of yours

and slow down."

Tanner handed him the bird food, and said, "I

would like to stay here. Whom do I talk to about finding a

room?"

The old man looked at him for a long moment. He

tied off the bag of birdseed and placed it in his jacket

pocket. He stood from the weathered park bench, and the

pigeons scattered. Elmer replied, "I have a small place in

the back of my house that I used to lease. You're welcome

to rent it until you find your way. Why don't we go across

the street to Mama's Café? Rosemary can fix us up a plate

of her famous homemade pot roast, and we'll talk about it."

16

Tanner moved into the tiny studio behind Elmer's house and then spent the greater part of a month looking for work in the sleepy village of sixteen thousand people. It was a rainy Friday night in early November. He decided to venture out of his small rental to search for a pulse in this town. Tanner found himself sitting on a stool in an old tavern; once a hotel, it had been converted into a bar— historical photos of the building and its people covered nearly every available wall space. The place was filled with lumber mill workers and anglers. It was payday, and their spirits were high.

This place has good energy, he thought.

Tanner was soon interrupted by a slap on his shoulder. He was greeted by a disheveled-looking, long-haired man, wearing a soiled University of Oregon sweatshirt. The sleeves were cut or torn off, it was hard to tell. He wore wrinkled brown shorts with a pair of old Birkenstocks. The man looked as if he'd just jumped out of bed. In a deep, slow voice, he greeted, "My name is Rick; welcome to the Tree House; not sure if I've met you before."

Tanner responded, "You haven't unless we picked peaches in West Texas together."

Rick took the seat beside him and raised a finger towards the bartender. A cold draft was immediately placed in front of him as he rested his elbows on the bar. "The curse of a small town is we know everyone's business," Rick chuckled. "How is old, Elmer? We don't see much of him anymore—great man. The entire town

looks after him. From my estimation, you are the red-

headed guy from Texas that lives in his mama's old

studio."

Tanner laughed, "You would be correct. Elmer is

doing well. We hit it off the moment we met. We talk a lot

about life, how to handle adversity, and how much he

misses Sophie and his family."

Rick boomed, "Good! Great to hear! What brings

you here?"

Tanner paused at the question and struggled with

his answer. *Do I give him the deep philosophical*

response, or do I just tell him I'm looking for work? he

wondered. He'd had a few drinks, so he decided on the

non-filtered incoherent response, "Well, I'm an

unemployed former peach picker and boxing champion

slash crab fisherman looking for a steady job that doesn't

involve being punched in the face or jumping into the

Bering Sea."

Rick interrupted, "Really? I don't know any crab fishermen, but I'm a huge boxing fan. I have big pay-per-view boxing events here at the Tree House. What's your name?"

Tanner slowly grimaced, knowing a reaction from Rick was forthcoming. "My name is Tanner Childress."

Rick closed his eyes, appearing to concentrate as he tried to recall that name. Then, he slapped his hand on the counter. The owner stood and shouted, "No way! Tanner Childress, the long shot winner in the Las Vegas tournament, who . . ." he paused.

Tanner dropped his head and winced, anticipating what Rick was going to say.

The bar owner became quiet. He raised his glass and gestured towards Tanner, and said, "You are one hell of a fighter, son." He finished his beer.

A tall, lanky patron wearing a cowboy hat and a

faded denim jacket shouted across the bar, "I'm tired of you cheating me out of my money!" He was yelling at the diminutive bartender, who was noticeably shaken by the bigger man's anger. He was clearly drunk and in a bad mood.

"I'm not paying for this!" he roared. The man's face was bright red as he repeated, "I'm not paying for this!"

A long pause from the bartender ensued, as the cowboy became more irritated.

He slammed his check on the table and looked fiercely at the bartender and shouted, "You know what; I think you are a thief—trying to steal my money! Do you know how hard I work for my money? Do you? I think I'll drag your butt outside and teach you a lesson!"

Rick rolled his eyes, shaking his head. "I'm so tired of that guy. He does this every payday. He clearly can't handle his alcohol." He sighed loudly as he walked around to behind the bar. He gestured to the bartender away from the conflict and focused on the drunken cowboy. The bartender quickly grabbed his keys. Rick looked at his employee briefly to comfort him, but the bartender had already exited through the back door. Rick was now in a sour mood; he spoke to the drunken patron in an annoying tone,, "What seems to be the problem?"

The cowboy was not happy with the owner's tone. His temper flared, and he said, "I don't like the way you just said that to me. Not only am I not paying this tab, but I'm going to kick your ass too!"

He pushed Rick, who nearly fell to the floor.

Tanner glanced around the bar. He noticed apprehension and fear on nearly everyone's faces. The young Texan jumped from his stool and hurried over to help Rick. "Hey, I think it's time for you to leave," Tanner interjected.

"I'm not going anywhere until I bust a foot in this

crook's ass!"

Tanner squeezed his arm tightly. The cowboy punched Tanner in the chest, which did nothing to affect Tanner's hold. The man's face turned red; he growled as Tanner stepped away from the cowboy's free arm. The cowboy tried to swing at Tanner's head several times, but the boxer avoided the flurry of swings and managed to sidestep behind him and grab hold of his other arm. Tanner kicked him in the calf, which made the guy drop to his knees.

Tanner then leaned over and calmly spoke into his ear, "I don't want to hurt you, but I want to be perfectly clear, I can hurt you badly! You will walk out of here; you will go home and sleep it off. If you ever want to come back in here again, you owe every one of us an apology. You can start with Rick."

The bar erupted with applause.

Still behind the cowboy, Tanner maintained his

grip, and then quickly lifted him off the floor and marched him out the front door. Tanner released his grip, watched the guy as he stumbled away for a few minutes, and then returned inside.

The bar was full of nervous chatter. Rick had turned on some music to temper the mood and was busy serving cocktails. After finishing the waitress' orders, he poured Tanner a drink and thanked him. "I understand you've been looking for work since you arrived in town last month?"

Tanner looked at him quizzically while shaking his head and laughing, "It *is* a small town, isn't it?"

Rick was wiping a glass and grinned at Tanner. "I need a bartender, and you need a job."

17

Emilia slowly pulled into the Tree House parking

lot. She'd had a rough morning with her three children.

The family had been in this country for nearly a year, and

her kids were already missing home. She quickly looked

at the car visor mirror—her makeup had smeared from

wiping her tears.

Emilia took a deep breath and muttered slowly,

"Okay, put yourself together. You didn't travel this far to

live your life as a sad loser." She reapplied her makeup

and fixed her hair. The former Miss Ecuador was a

beautiful woman.

Emilia was a widow. Her husband had suffered from a drug abuse problem and eventually had died from an overdose. Emilia could certainly let a man care for her, but this time, she swore loudly, "I'm going to succeed my way. I'll talk with the kids tomorrow morning—we are going to be winners!"

Emilia exited her car and with a determined look, she entered through the back door of the Tree House bar.

The kitchen staff greeted her with the familiar, *"Buenos Dias"* and *"Hola."* The men adored her—she always carried herself with dignity. The cooks would routinely offer her food and invite her and her kids to family gatherings, but she politely refused. She learned long ago to be careful not to encourage men.

It was late Sunday afternoon, and the bar was filled with people watching American football. Emilia knew nothing about the game, nor did she have any interest in watching sports.

The lovely Ecuadorian noticed the new bartender. He was all muscles with a head full of red hair. He was leaning over the bar top and appeared to be flirting with one of the women.

She shook her head, "Great—another *pendejo*." She whispered, "I need to make my money; I hope he knows what he is doing."

Emilia approached a table of fishermen. They were drunk as well as lacking any filters.

One of them shouted, "Emilia!" He stood up and tried to hug her. He stank of stale beer and dirty clothes.

She stepped back looking troubled, and said, "Robert, you need a shower plus a nap!"

The table roared with laughter. He put his hands up in the air, quickly dropped them to his side, and sat down. He laughed with his friends; and then asked the Ecuadorian beauty, "Do you work on Tuesdays?"

"Yes, why Robert?" she replied annoyingly.

"Well, I shower on Tuesdays," he joked.

She laughed along with the fishermen. They ordered drinks and Emilia made her way back to the waitress' station.

Tanner, still leaning over the bar, listened as the troubled woman lamented the unexpected loss of her mother several weeks ago. He felt saddened. Tanner understood her anguish. It was taking her some time to finish the story, but he was sensitive about interrupting her.

Emilia stared over at the new bartender. She waited several minutes before calling to him, "Excuse me! I need some service."

Without turning, Tanner held his hand out acknowledging that he'd heard her but was still busy.

The poor lady would not stop talking. Apparently, her mother had lived with her and had helped raise her kids while working. They had been close. She was a big influence in her children's life. Tanner tried to interject, but the woman would not stop talking.

A few more minutes passed, Emilia had had enough. She shouted, "Hey! Asshole! I have customers who are waiting for their drinks."

This got his attention, and Tanner lifted his elbows off the bar. The woman stopped talking and took a drink of her cocktail. He turned towards the waitress; his face was fiery red, and he scowled at her, and asked, "How can I help you?"

Tanner's tone only made Emilia more upset. The guy was flirting with a customer, and she needed to service hers before they decided to leave. She shouted loudly in Spanish, *"¿No tienes idea cómo hacer este trabajo?* (You have no idea how to do this job, do you?) *¡Coqueteas con los clients e ignores tu trabajo!* (You flirt with the customers and ignore your job!)." She reached over the bar, ripped the drink order from the printer, and slammed it on the counter. She continued to shout in Spanish, *"¡Haz estas bebidas y deja de ser un pendejo!* (Now make these drinks and stop being an asshole!)"

Tanner's body began to shake. He tried breathing in deeply to keep himself from losing his temper. Emilia stared at him sternly as Tanner poured the draft beers and filled the shot glasses. She reached for the tray filled with drinks when he was finished, but Tanner quickly pressed his hands against the tray. He'd had time to think about what he wanted to say, *"Ahora que has terminado con tu rabieta, tengo algo importante que decirte* (Now that you are finished with your tantrum, I have something important to tell you.)"

Emilia's eyes widened in shock that he was speaking to her in Spanish. Her lips straightened, and her back stiffened.

Tanner looked over at the grieving woman, who was staring at her drink, he then quickly returned his gaze to Emilia. He continued, *"Ese cliente está sufriendo la muerte de su madre. Ella es más importante que alimentar bebidas a una mesa llena de pescadores borrachos* (That customer is grieving the death of her mother. She is more important than feeding more drinks to a table filled with drunk fishermen.)" Tanner released the tray and snapped, "You may be the most beautiful woman I've ever seen on the outside, but your insides are ugly."

Her face turned red as she cried out, "No! You don't know me!" She then grabbed one of the shots from the tray and downed it, slamming the glass on the counter, and said, "I need this refilled."

Tanner paused for a moment; he was at a loss for words. The young Texan shook his head and turned away from her to refill the glass.

Emilia continued to glare at him. Tanner returned

the drink to the tray.

Then, he said quietly, "Here you go."

The waitress was not finished with him. She

grabbed the refilled glass and finished it.

"I need another," the young Ecuadorian tossed the

tumbler at his chest.

He managed to catch the glass. Tanner softly set it

in the sink and retrieved a fresh glass.

He struggled to comment, "You, ugh ..." He let out

a deep sigh, filled the glass, and now held the bottle in his

hand, ready to pour another. Her scowl turned to a smirk

as she walked away with her tray.

Tanner just stared at her, still at a loss for words.

His stomach began to ache as his heart raced.

Emilia returned with an empty tray and another

order. Then, in her Spanish accent, she said, "Well, now

that I have your attention, I need . . . "

The bartender interrupted, "Can we start over?" he

pleaded. "My name is Tanner. I just moved here."

"You have a funny accent, Tanner. Where are you from?"

Tanner felt relieved. They were talking civilly.

"Texas," he replied. He placed a full pint of beer onto her tray.

Emilia picked up the pint and took a long drink. Tanner rolled his eyes as he poured another glass of beer and set it on the tray.

"Tanner from Texas. Is that where you learned to speak Spanish?" she smiled at him.

They looked at each other for a long, awkward moment.

"Yes, I learned Spanish on the farm back home. Where are you from? Mexico?"

"NO! Not from Mexico!" she animated. Emilia continued to drink from the customer's pint glass. "Why do all of you gringos think we are from Mexico! We have a different accent than Mexicans. I am from Ecuador!" she said proudly.

Tanner's hair stood straight up. Ignacio was from Ecuador.

Emilia noticed the surprised look on his face.

She asked, "What's wrong, Tanner? You don't like Ecuadorians?"

Tanner stepped away from his thoughts and returned to the conversation. The bartender shook his head and replied, "No, that's not it. It's just . . . it's just . . ." he hesitated, "Will you have dinner with me?"

Emilia slowly smiled; she reached out and tugged at his beard, and asked, "What is this mess?"

The Ecuadorian grabbed her tray and walked towards her table.

18

Tanner rubbed his hands across his freshly shaven

face. It had been months since he had a haircut. Emilia

had finally agreed to a date with him. They planned to

have dinner underneath an old sequoia redwood

overlooking the Pacific Ocean.

Tanner walked out of the small cottage behind

Elmer's place. The smell of pine trees with the forest

filled his lungs. It was deathly quiet except for the sound

of dried pine needles underneath his feet. The night was

cold; ice had begun to form on the undersides of trees and

cover the walkways. He looked over at Elmer's house before stepping into his car. He noticed Elmer was sitting in his rocking chair on the front porch and heard the faint sounds of a radio. He decided to say hello before leaving on his date.

Tanner approached the front porch; there were sounds of cheers from the radio along with Elmer shouting out into the night, "For crying out loud, play some defense!"

Tanner walked up the creaky, wooden steps. Elmer wore a red-and-black checkered flannel shirt, black leather boots, and faded jeans.

He turned the radio off and pushed his wavy, gray hair back from his face to greet his tenant. "Tanner! Look at you! You shaved and cut your hair!" He was overcome with joy. The old man smiled as he stomped his boot onto the wooden deck floor, and said, "Aww! You have a date, don't you?" He leaned back and laughed.

The older man closed his eyes, taking a sip from his tumbler of scotch on ice. Elmer lowered the drink and shook the glass; the familiar rattle of ice cubes reminded him he needed a refill.

Tanner rubbed his chin, chuckling as he admitted, "I do have a date. Nothing gets by you, Elmer."

Elmer leaned over from his rocking chair and picked up a half-empty bottle of scotch. He grinned, "Well, I'd love to take credit for that, but I knew you had a date with Emilia." He winked at Tanner, and said, "Welcome to the town of everybody's up in your business. I want you to take my car tonight, son." Elmer stretched his legs and groaned as he reached for the car keys in his pocket. "Aww, there they are!" The older man pulled out his set of keys, which slipped from his hand and fell onto the deck. Elmer had obviously finished more than a few glasses of scotch on ice that evening. "Take my truck, son. It has four-wheel drive. The year's first snowfall will arrive in a few hours."

Tanner picked up the keys and raised them towards him, and said, "Thank you, Elmer; I'll put gas in it."

Elmer sarcastically laughed. "Ha, where? This town has already shut down." Then his face became serious, as he added, "This may be the only place in the world where someone has died of boredom."

He clutched his stomach while laughing and rocked quickly back and forth in his chair. His cheeks had a bright red blush from the scotch and the freezing temperature.

Tanner soaked in Elmer's antics, which lightened his heart. He waited for Elmer to finish and then replied, "Thank you."

Elmer stopped rocking, his eyes glowed. He nodded slowly and said, "Keep this in mind tonight. My Sophie used to say to me, treat our relationship as if it is the most delicate flower freshly picked from the forest that is so fragile it may die in your hands before reaching home."

Tanner mused, "Why the forest?"

Elmer replied, "This flower was not deliberately planted in your garden; it's a gift from the forest—a living part of our Universe. A picked flower needs to be patiently nurtured." Elmer continued, "Have you met Hipatia and the kids?"

"No, not yet?"

"Well, you're in for a treat. Those kids are special. They love their mother. Sebastian, Omar, and Ivana are the sweetest children I've ever met. Now Hipatia is widowed—she lost her husband when Emilia was just a toddler." Elmer settled back in his chair and stared into the night, and said, "I think that really had an impact on Emilia." He took a drink and chewed on a piece of ice.

"I understand, Elmer."

Elmer nodded as the sound of him chewing ice filled the porch.

"Thank you, Elmer."

The old Scottish man waved goodbye as Tanner left the porch.

He started the truck and made his way towards town. Tall pines, cedar with giant redwoods bordered the road on both sides. He lowered the window to smell the brisk ocean air mixed with the scents of the old-growth forest. It was the best of both worlds. After a few minutes, he entered the town of Whisper. He stopped to pick up the warm Italian take-out and made his way to Emilia's place.

Tanner pulled into the driveway. His heart quickened and his stomach ached. The frigid ocean breeze and his nervous energy made Tanner shake. His hands turned cold, and he shoved them in his jacket as he approached the well-lit and freshly painted, white wooden-framed house. The front door quickly opened, and an adorable young boy with big, round, brown eyes, olive skin, and a wide grin greeted him. He had straight, thin hair and a chubby, little stomach. The little guy looked up at the muscular man and said with a heavy Spanish accent, "Whoa, you are big!"

The door was then opened further by Emilia's mother, Hipatia. She had beautiful, red hair, green eyes, and a warm, loving smile. She chuckled in response to the young boy's greeting. Hipatia tousled her grandson's hair, looked up at Tanner, and said, "Hola Tanner."

The young boy, Omar, repeated his *abuela's* words. "Hola Tanner," he said, still grinning.

Tanner smiled back at Omar and reached out his hand, and said, "You must be Omar, the parrot."

Omar shook Tanner's hand and giggled, "You must be Omar, the parrot."

The soothing sound of a piano could be heard from

inside the house and Tanner paused to listen.

Hipatia beamed, "That is my grandson, Sebastian.

He plays beautifully, doesn't he?"

"*Si* Hipatia, *que maravilloso (Yes, Hipatia, how*

beautiful)" Tanner said, as he placed his hand on his

heart.

She nodded silently. Tanner saw Emilia walk into

the room, and the music stopped abruptly. Soon Emilia

and her son Sebastian approached the front door. Tanner's

mouth opened, and his heart raced as she drew closer.

Sebastian could sense the man's anxiety. The young boy

started to laugh and jump. Emilia nervously held onto him

more tightly. Her eyes sparkled when she noticed Tanner

had shaved his beard.

"You shaved that dirty animal off your face! You

look good, gringo!" she said approvingly. "This is my son,

Sebastian," she said, as she rubbed his neck; the young

boy waved as he rested his head against his mother's side.

Tanner leaned over to shake his hand, and said, "Hello, Sebastian. I loved listening to you play the piano."

"Thank you," the boy said shyly, "do you play an instrument?"

"I do! Well, I try. It has been a very long time since I played." Tanner motioned with his hands, and added, "I play the guitar."

Sebastian lifted his head from his mother's side, and said, "Really? We should play!"

Emilia kissed her son and squeezed him as she shouted towards the back of the house, "Ivanita! Please come here!"

Ivana's eyes were puffy. She looked as if she had been crying and appeared disinterested. She had her mother's beauty but was clearly suffering. Ivana responded in a thick Spanish accent. "Hello Tanner, nice to meet you," she said, trying to raise her hand.

Her mother was annoyed. "Oh Ivana, stop it! We

will talk some more when I get home!"

They stepped back inside from the front door and started whispering. Tanner could not make out what was said, but he was sure they were fighting.

Emilia soon appeared; she kissed her mother and the boys and moved quickly towards Elmer's truck, and said, "Let's get out of here!"

Tanner started the vehicle and slowly backed out of the driveway.

Emilia started, "So, you met my family? Tell me about yours."

He explained the fate of his sister. It took so long to share the story that they found that they had parked underneath a redwood tree and spent nearly an hour there. The food was cold.

Emilia was crying for Aimee. The Ecuadorian took a deep breath while wiping tears from her eyes. She said solemnly, "My grandma used to say, even the deepest wounds eventually scar."

Tanner reached towards the backseat for the brown bag with food and wine. He managed to pull out the bottle, and then turned on the cab light to find the corkscrew on the truck's console.

He opened the bottle of cabernet, paused, and then shouted, "Oh No!"

"What happened? What?" Emilia raised her voice in concern, and she straightened up in her seat.

Tanner laughed, shaking his head, and admitted, "I forgot the wine glasses."

Emilia looked at him with a smile. Then, she laughed softly, and said, "Gringo, you are a mess." She placed her hand on his forearm. "You know what my grandma also said?" she asked, her thick Spanish accent turning sultry.

Tanner laughed again, and asked, "What did she say?"

Emilia grabbed the bottle of wine from Tanner, lifted it to her mouth, and took a long swig. Then, she lowered the bottle, wiping her lips with the palm of her hand, and said, "Don't let the details ruin a good party."

They both laughed loudly. Tanner grabbed the bottle from Emilia and took a long drink. He passed the wine back to her. They soon noticed droplets on the windshield.

Emilia looked at him and then towards the front of the car. "Turn on the headlights, Tanner."

He did and small, powdery chunks of snow slowly fell around them. Emilia turned excited. She opened the car door to step in front of the truck.

Tanner followed her.

The forest was quiet. It was as if the forest creatures had also stopped to admire the first winter snowfall. Tanner stood under the giant redwood sequoias—being surrounded by trees and the ocean made sense to him. He believed that living among the rows of manicured lawns, concrete paths, and traffic sounds made us toxic and confused.

Tanner took a deep breath, and said, "I love the smell of the forest."

Emilia's hair was sprinkled with dabs of white snowflakes. He moved closer to her, and she turned her body away from him. She was nervous.

He leaned over, kissed the top of her head, and said, "Isn't this beautiful?"

She turned back, her face glowing. "It's perfect!" She put her arms around him, still holding the half-empty wine bottle in one hand and kissed him. Her heart raced and she reminded herself that she needed to take her time. Emilia pushed away from him. "You know what my grandma says?" she asked quizzically.

Tanner chuckled, "I can only imagine."

"Don't make fun of my grandma, gringo! She is

my inspiration!" Emilia retorted.

"No, I'm not!" Tanner's smile was so broad that his mouth was completely open. "What did she say?"

Emilia took a long drink of the wine, nearly finishing the bottle. She wiped the corner of her mouth as she started to walk towards the truck. Miss Ecuador replied loudly, "It's time to put the cork back in the bottle when you confuse hormones with love."

She stood on the doorstep of the truck and waved him towards Elmer's truck, and said, "Take me home, gringo!"

Tanner shook his head playfully. He continued to smile and mumbled softly, "Yes, ma'am."

19

Kenny walked into the dining room wearing black slacks, a pressed, white Oxford shirt, and a dinner vest. Aimee was working on her laptop at the table. She looked up and jumped excitedly from her chair.

She signed, "Let me look at you."

She straightened her father's collar and wiped some lint off his jacket.

"Thank you, sweetheart. I don't want to look like a complete mess on my date with Stacey. Are you doing your homework?"

Aimee shook her head and smiled as she walked back to the dining room table.

Kenny waited patiently for his daughter to explain.

She waved her father over to look at the computer screen.

Kenny read out loud, "Complete tongue replacement surgery. What—I can't believe it!" Kenny shouted.

Aimee giggled and jumped in the air.

"When we looked at having the surgery years ago, the doctor said you risked a severe infection from the surgery. And we have the money!" Kenny celebrated. The moment was too much for him and he fell to his knees. "I need some water, Aimee. I'm super dizzy."

Aimee rushed into the kitchen, returned with a glass of water, and handed it to him.

Kenny finished the drink, gave the glass to his daughter, and attempted to slow his breathing.

He finally stood, straightened his clothes, and studied his beautiful daughter. He could see his child becoming whole. It made his heart accelerate.

"Find out when and where you can have the surgery. I'll make the calls and take you anywhere in the world to make this happen for you, honey." Kenny walked to his daughter and gave her a long, loving hug. Then, he placed his hands on her shoulders.

Aimee had a twinkle in her eyes, causing Kenny to laugh joyfully.

"I'm going to meet Stacey for dinner. Let's make the arrangements in the morning."

Aimee nodded. She kissed her father on the cheek, stepped back, and waved goodbye.

20

Kenny and Stacey settled into a comfortable,

strawberry-colored, upholstered booth. The table was

covered with a white lace tablecloth accented with candles

as a trio of musicians played in the background. Gloria's

was dimly lit, making for the perfect ambiance to share an

intimate evening away from home.

"Stacey, you look beautiful tonight."

Stacey smiled widely. She was wearing a dark

green, sequined velvet dress. Her strawberry blonde hair

was styled in a half-up bouffant with S-shaped curls

resting against her shoulders.

They were eating lasagna and sharing a nice bottle of cabernet.

Kenny took a drink from his glass of wine. He looked at Stacey, and confessed, "I think this is our sixth date since we met at group therapy."

Stacey sat back and placed the silverware on her plate. She sipped her wine and grinned, "And?"

"Well, it seems that you're always the one asking me questions. I appreciate that you have taken an interest in me and my life, but I'm very curious about something. I think it will reveal a lot about you."

Stacey took another sip of her wine. She leaned forward, placing her elbows on the table, and whispered, "What is it you want to know?"

"I know you have been divorced and are a widow, but I'd like to know *why* you are divorced."

Stacey took a bite of her food and held up a finger

indicating that she would respond in a moment. After a sip of wine, she was ready to answer. "My ex-husband was a narcissist and an alcoholic. He was incapable of loving me because he didn't have the capacity to understand love. Our sex life was horrible. When he was finished, we were finished. When something went wrong, it was my fault. It was my fault he drank. It was my fault when I spent too much time with our kids and not with him. For some reason, going to my daughter's soccer practice was selfish when I should have been spending that time with him at a bar. Day after day, I watched him take every conversation, every detail that involved me, and make it about himself. When my mother died, he literally collapsed in a theatrical grieving episode at my mother's wake, and once again made it about himself. I never forgave him for that, I was so hurt. I lost whatever self-esteem I had left.

She looked at Kenny and continued, "I was saved by a man who shared what a relationship should look like.

I had an affair. His sweetness and sincere, loving expressions reminded me of what I had lost."

Stacey took another sip of wine. She exhaled, "When I say 'loving expressions,' I mean everything from being a good listener to just holding my hand. Everything felt perfect. I divorced my narcissistic ex-husband and began dating someone who truly respected me. We dated for several years before deciding to marry. A few months after we got married, he died of a blood clot in his sleep."

Kenny looked troubled. Stacey's face showed her stress.

"I am so sorry, Stace. I will never treat you that way. I wouldn't treat anyone that way."

Stacey smiled softly, "I know. It was why I asked you to have coffee with me. I listened to your beautiful sentimental words during our group therapy session, and your story moved me. All I could think of was wanting to have that kind of relationship. I want to feel that depth of love and kindness." She reached across the table and held his hands, and said, "You are very special, Kenny Childress. If we're lucky, maybe we can share a lifetime of selfless acts of kindness, sentimental expressions of love, and who knows?" Stacey grabbed her fork, looked down at her plate, and then playfully with her mouth full of food, she added, "And some great sex."

Kenny blushed.

Stacey continued, "It's my turn to ask you a question. We've been on six dates, had daily phone calls, and intimate conversations that make us feel closer, yet you haven't even kissed me. Why? Are you not feeling it? Am I not attractive enough for you?"

Kenny shook his head, his eyebrows raised. "Oh no, that's not it!" he said excitedly. "I haven't dated in so long, Stacey. I don't even know where to start."

A rendition of *Careless Whisper* by George Michael filled the restaurant.

Stacey giggled, "Perfect—come on, dance with me."

Kenny and Stacey made their way to the empty dance floor. They embraced and slowly danced to the rhythm of the song. They looked into each other's eyes. They were falling in love. Kenny touched her cheek. She turned and kissed his hand. Kenny leaned towards Stacey and kissed her as they stopped dancing and held each other in a tight embrace. When the song ended, the band stopped and turned to each other. A feeling of joy filled the trio.

Finally, they stopped kissing. Stacey looked up at him to read his facial expression after their first kiss. Kenny inhaled a deep breath of relief.

The lead singer announced, "Give it up for the two lovebirds!"

The restaurant broke out in applause and whistles.

They laughed.

He grabbed her hand and walked her off the dance floor.

21

"Oh Lordy, mama! That looks amazing!" Emilia praised. "What do you think, Tanner?"

"It looks good, and it smells good," he replied. Hipatia, Emilia's mother, placed the large roasted turkey at the center of the table.

Tanner turned to Emilia, and asked, "Can you cook like this?"

The Ecuadorian scoffed, "Are you looking for a maid or a lover?"

Her children laughed. Sebastian commented, "No,

mom is a horrible cook."

Hipatia announced, "Happy Thanksgiving,

everyone! Our first holiday with Tanner! In celebration, I

have combined the best of foods from both our countries."

She had made the traditional turkey, stuffing, and

brown gravy, but had added *ceviche, aji de queso,* and

fanesca. Latin music played softly in the background.

Everyone was in good spirits except for Ivana. Her eyes

were puffy, and she appeared disinterested.

Hipatia sat down at one end of the table. She took

a sip of her wine and looked at all her blessings. Her eyes

fell on her granddaughter, Ivana, and she squeezed her

wrists, *"Mi hita,* please say grace."

Ivana moaned, "Grandma, no . . . "

Hipatia leaned over and whispered into her ear.

Ivana straightened in her chair and Hipatia smiled with

great joy. "Tanner, I want to share a prayer my mother

used to say on special occasions. It is a prayer from our

ancestors."

Hipatia, the kids, and Emilia bowed their heads.

To the winds of the South

Great Serpent

Thank you for the healing light you bring to us

For helping us to shed the deadness of our past the

way you shed your skin, all at once

Thank you for teaching us the Beauty Way.

To the winds of the West

Mother Sister Jaguar

Thank you for protecting our medicine space

We embrace your wisdom of teaching us the ways

Of peace, impeccability, and the journey beyond

death.

To the winds of the North

Hummingbird, Grandmothers, and Grandfathers

Ancient Ones

Thank you for sharing this space with us

We listen for your whispers to us in the wind and

to the sacred space within our hearts.

Guide us with your grace.

To the winds of the East

Great Eagle, Condor

Thank you for taking us upon your wings to our

highest path of destiny

Thank you for showing us the holy mountains and

reminding us to envision our lives from this place.

Mother Earth

Pachamama

We give you thanks, as one of your children, for

holding us so sweetly in your womb of love and life as we

heal all of our stories, our shadows, our fears.

Father Sun, Grandmother Moon

Star Nations—Star Brothers and Sisters

Great Spirit

You who are known by a thousand names

The unnamable, the nameless one

You who are unknown, yet not unknowable

Thank you for bringing us together

And allowing us to sing the song of Life, one more

day.

Emilia's mother raised her head. She then rubbed her hands together, and praised, *"Bon appétite!"*

"That was a nice prayer, Hipatia. I was a little nervous when you started with '*great serpent*,' but the prayer ended beautifully," Tanner confessed.

Hipatia laughed, "Oh, the snake is not a demon to the Incan people. It represents new life. With new life, comes wisdom and knowledge."

"Do you believe in the Christian faith? Tanner asked.

Sebastian held his plate up towards his grandmother as she carved the turkey.

She replied, "I do believe in the Christian faith. I

also honor my heritage by sharing a prayer close to my family."

Emilia interjected, "From my grandma, Tanner! Oh, you know, my inspiration!"

Emilia and her mother laughed. They loved Emilia's grandmother. She was very smart and very funny.

"Grandma was always filling our hearts with love and wisdom."

Ivana's plate remained empty. She still appeared sad and tired.

Tanner boldly asked the young woman, "What is wrong, Ivana? What seems to be bothering you?"

Ivana's gaze remained on her empty plate. She started to slowly rock in her chair.

Emilia interrupted, "My angel is upset from losing her boyfriend." Emilia stared compassionately at her oldest child. "Did you throw up again this morning, *mi*

197

hija?"

"Yes, mama," she rubbed her eyes, and said, "I'm tired of feeling this way."

Tanner interjected, "I remember what my high school teacher used to say when someone experienced a separation or a loss. She would say: *The emptiness you feel inside is you making room for someone special to fill it.*

"Awe I like that, gringo," Emilia said.

Ivana looked at him and smiled. Then, the young woman started to fill her plate with *ceviche.*

"Tanner, we have a guitar!" Sebastian blurted, his legs swinging with excitement, occasionally hitting the underside of the dinner table with his sneakers.

Tanner's heart filled with joy, and he said, "I can't wait to play! Let's eat so fast that we skip chewing our food so we can start playing!"

Everyone at the table laughed. Emilia grabbed

Tanner's wrist, and said, "Hush, gringo!"

The Ecuadorian mama turned to her son, and said, "*Mijo*, take your time. We are looking forward to listening to you play for us."

"Do you fish? I want to go fishing?" asked the chubby boy with big brown eyes as he smiled at Tanner.

"I do know how to fish, Omar! I have not fished around here, but I bet we could figure out how. Would you like to go on Sunday?"

Omar's broad smile forced his eyes to squint as he said softly, "Yes."

Emilia interrupted, "He has never fished before. You will have to teach him."

Tanner had finished filling his plate with food. "Does anyone else want to go fishing this Sunday?"

The others replied, "No."

They laughed and continued filling their plates.

"Okay, Omarcito, that gives us three days to figure

out where, what, when, and how to fish Whisper Lake,"

Tanner boasted.

Omar bounced in his chair. The boy loved his

food. He was nine years old, his brother, Sebastian, was

eleven, and Ivana was sixteen. Tanner had no idea how

old Emilia was until he sneaked into her purse and looked

at her passport. She gave him a different age every time he

asked. She was thirty-one. Tanner was twenty-eight.

Emilia would occasionally mimic the song in the

background, playfully changing the tone of her voice to

make her rendition sound comical. The kids laughed

between bites of food. Tanner wore a big smile.

Dinner was officially over when Grandma Hipatia

stood up from the table. That was Sebastian's cue, and he

raced across the room to sit in front of his piano. Tanner

helped Emilia and Hipatia clear the dishes. They started

washing plates and platters, but Sebastian called for

Tanner to join him. Emilia kissed Tanner's cheek and

rubbed his back, then, she whispered, "Go be with my

son; mom and I can finish up here."

Tanner walked into the living room and found a

guitar case resting against the side of the sofa. He opened

the case and admired the guitar. He whispered, "An old

Martin acoustic guitar. Wow!"

Sebastian turned in his chair to watch Tanner's

expression.

"This is nice, Sebastian!" he complimented. "It's

been a while since I've played." Tanner picked at the

strings.

Sebastian smiled and said, "I already tuned the

guitar. Tell me a song you know, and I will play with

you."

"Any song?" Tanner asked sarcastically.

"Do you know *Stairway to Heaven?*"

Tanner laughed and started to stumble through the

chords.

Sebastian rubbed his chin while he listened. Then, he turned to the piano and began playing. The young boy stopped to listen to Tanner for a while longer. The redhead struggled to maintain a tempo. Sebastian looked up the tablature online and placed the digital music sheet in front of him. Within a few moments, Sebastian could play the song without hesitation. The Texan stopped playing and listened to the child prodigy as he performed *Stairway to Heaven* on his piano.

Sebastian stopped a few minutes later, and said, "You are not playing, Tanner!"

Tanner began to sing while Sebastian played the piano. Hipatia and Emilia stopped washing the dishes and peeked into the living room.

Omar wanted to join. He stood between Sebastian and Tanner and tried singing in a hip-hop beatbox style. He turned his hips from side to side, and sang, "Yo, yo, boom, pt, boom, to heaven, yo to heaven."

Everyone laughed hysterically.

They played a few more songs before Tanner returned the guitar to the case. He reached for the remote to turn on the television. He'd watched the Dallas Cowboys play football on Thanksgiving for as long as he could remember.

Emilia shouted from the kitchen, "Whatcha doin, gringo?"

"Turning on the football game," Tanner replied.

"Oh no, Tanner! Turn the television off and help me move the furniture," she demanded.

"Are we vacuuming?" Tanner asked playfully.

"Mama, turn up the volume!" The sounds of salsa filled the room and Emilia shook her hips, "No, it's time to celebrate, gringo!"

Everyone began to dance. Emilia, Hipatia, and Tanner emptied a few bottles of wine as they continued dancing into the night. Finally, even Emilia seemed to be getting tired. That was Tanner's cue to leave. He made his

way towards Emilia to wish her good night. They

embraced and shared a long, romantic kiss.

Tanner whispered to her, "Thank you—thank you

for everything."

He walked towards the door when Emilia interrupted,

"Where do you think you're going?"

22

"Is that a fish!" Omar shouted.

"Shh, no, Marcito, it is the minnow swimming."

Tanner pressed his hand against the boy's arm, and said,

"You must keep your voice down. We will scare the fish

away."

"Oh, okay, okay," he whispered. Omar held the

rod with one hand and fidgeted with the reel in his other

hand.

"Let me see your fishing rod."

Omar handed it to Tanner. His eyes never left sight

of the bobber. Tanner leaned the fishing pole against the ice chest. He placed rocks around the bottom of the rod to keep it secured. "You will know when you have a fish biting your minnow. That bobber will go underwater; as soon as it does, just wait about five seconds and gently lift the rod towards you and reel in your fish," Tanner explained.

Omar sat on the ground and rubbed his fingers through the moistened dirt.

Tanner sat next to him.

The young boy asked, "What do we do now?"

Tanner chuckled, "We wait."

The Texan pointed towards the bobber, and said, "That big fish will swim around that minnow." Tanner inhaled through his nose, and added, "He will smell that delicious minnow."

Omar giggled.

"He is then going to look at that minnow. Make

sure that he doesn't have anything sick growing on him," Tanner became more animated. "And then boom!" he whispered. His eyes widened, and he licked his lips, "That big, old, fat fish will devour our minnow."

Omar chuckled, "He'll just swallow him whole!"

Tanner laughed with him, "Yes, that big, fat, lazy fish will swallow him whole."

"Does the fish say grace?" Omar asked.

"Hmm, well, I don't think so. However, I do believe the very act of fish eating food is part of the universal grace bestowed on all of us. If you look at the world this way, you do not have to look far to see the blessings God has given us." Tanner patted the young boy on the back.

"What about my father? Why did God take him away from me? I don't feel blessed."

Omar leaned over, drawing figures on the ground with a stick.

Tanner's stomach turned. He understood this question. It was the same one he'd asked himself for many years.

"Well, that is a very difficult question, Omar. First, let me tell you that your father has not left you. He is still inside your heart. You have his blood pumping inside of you. No one knows God's design. People claim they do, but how can we begin to understand a God that can make a place like earth? What if your papa is watching us? Do we really know? What if he is that fat finch looking at us from that tree branch?"

Omar smiled and waved at the bird.

"I feel that Omar Guevara was placed on this planet at the right time and the right place. A divine purpose is growing inside of you. Do not let the world change who you are. Listen to your heart. Let it guide you. Perhaps someday, losing your father will make sense. By that time, if you listen to yourself and pay attention to the messages, you will become this amazing superhero soul."

Omar stood up, excited, and asked, "Do you really think so? How will I know when I receive messages?"

Tanner pointed towards the bobber, and said, "Omar!"

Omar quickly grabbed the fishing rod from between the rocks and gently lifted the pole. He was a natural, Tanner thought. The young boy steadily reeled the line into his spool. The fish jumped above the surface, slapped its tail against the water, and then dove deep into the depths of Whisper Lake. Omar tried to reel it in, but the fish kept dragging more line from the spool.

Tanner shouted, "Let him take the line. Don't worry, he'll tire soon. Keep your tip up."

Within a few moments, the sound of the fishing line leaving the rod stopped abruptly. Omar began reeling the fish towards him; his rod was nearly arcing in a semi-circle. This time, Omar was able to bring the fish close to shore.

"That is a good-sized rainbow, Omar! At least three pounds!"

Tanner grabbed the net, but the fish spooked. The sound of the fishing line being dragged from the reel caused Omar to laugh. The boy patiently waited until the fish stopped swimming. As soon as the trout paused, Omar pulled his rod towards him and began reeling. The fish splashed in the shallow waters. Omar stepped farther away from the shore to drag his catch closer to Tanner's net.

"I got it!" Tanner called.

Omar dropped the pole and ran towards Tanner. The Texan moved as far as he could from the shore. He did not want to accidentally drop the fish into the water. "You did it, Omar! What a beautiful fish!"

Omar's beamed and grabbed the fish with both hands, and it immediately fell from his clutches. Tanner picked the fish up off the ground by placing his fingers underneath the jawbone and holding its tail. "This is how you hold this beauty," Tanner demonstrated.

Omar grabbed the fish accordingly. He held it in front of him. His eyes filled with joy.

Tanner reached for his cell phone and took a picture. "Let's get this baby on a stringer and try catching another one!" Tanner boasted.

A few hours passed. Omar managed to catch a few smaller trout. The young boy was tired from all the excitement and ready to go home. Tanner taught him how to clean and prepare the fish for dinner.

They made their way to the car. The two were greeted by a group of older men with fishing gear getting a late start. "Did you catch anything?" one of them asked.

Omar stuck his chest out and lowered his voice, and said, "I caught all these!"

The men smiled, "Well, you will have to teach us

next time!"

The two fishermen, Tanner and Omar, loaded their gear and made their way back to the Guevara house.

Omar broke the silence, "You said I need to listen to the messages. How do I do that?"

"Are you sure you're only nine years old?" Tanner joked. "Before I answer that, can you tell me why you need to listen to your messages?"

Omar replied, "They will make me a superhero!"

Tanner chuckled, "Well, yes. I think, more importantly, it will bring you closer to understanding who you are. If someone kindly shares with you bits of wisdom that will aid in your personal growth, be sure to listen. If you need help with decisions in your life and you ask God for his help, listen to his message. It may arrive through nature or from a stranger or even a book! Trust that you are part of something divine. If you can do that, I think you will be a great loving soul."

"Like you?" Omar asked.

Tanner's shoulders slumped and his eyes swelled.

He choked, "I'm trying, Omar. I still have a long path

ahead of me. But having you here with me today gives me

hope."

23

"*¡Mamá, no quiero estar embarazada!* (I don't want to be pregnant!)" Ivana shouted.

Sebastian's arms were wrapped around his sister as he leaned his head against her shoulder. Hipatia was sitting on her other side, rubbing her head. Emilia sat on a chair across from Ivana, her face was red, legs crossed, and arms folded. She shouted back, "Well, my love, you are pregnant! If you had listened to my advice, you would not be in this situation!"

Hipatia's face soured. She retorted, "You are one

to talk! You were younger than Ivana when you were pregnant with her."

"Mama, I know, I did not bring my children here to become losers!"

"Maria Emilia, hush! How can you say that?" Hipatia gasped.

Emilia's arms remained folded as tears began to form in her eyes. They were interrupted by the sound of the front door slamming against the wall.

Omar rushed into the house with his fishing pole; he called, "Mama, I caught three fish!"

He leaned over the side of the chair, and asked, "Can we cook them for dinner, mommy?"

Emilia touched her son's head, "Yes, of course, *mi amor,* let me finish with Ivana first."

Omar turned towards his sister, Sebastian, and his grandma. He noticed Ivana was crying. He dropped his fishing pole and kneeled in front of her. He clutched her legs, and asked, "What happened?"

Tanner had followed through the front door and could see that something was wrong. He stepped quietly over to Emilia and kissed her on the cheek, and whispered, "I'll get this fish ready for supper."

"I'm pregnant, *mijo,*" Ivana cried.

"Pregnant? Awesome!" the young boy celebrated.

"No, Marcito, not awesome. I am too young. I have so much I want to do," she explained.

Tanner was listening from the kitchen, his heart was racing. The poor girl was facing a very important decision.

"Have you told the jerk that you're pregnant?" Emilia asked.

Ivana whined, "No, Mama. He is not living here anymore. His father is in the military. I told you, they are overseas. I see from his photos online that he already has another girlfriend."

Emilia paused, "Well, what are you going to do?"

"I don't know. I want to be a writer. I want to do something important but raising a child will ruin my dreams—just like I ruined yours." Ivana rushed to her mother, and they held each other for a long time.

"No, my love. You did not ruin my life. You are my inspiration. Without you, I would have never been the woman I am now." Emilia placed her hands on Ivana's shoulders and leaned her forehead against her daughter's, and said, "I cannot imagine a life without you."

Tanner walked into the living room. Ivana and her mother turned to face him.

"Welcome to my world," Emilia joked.

Tanner nodded respectfully, sensitive to the gravity of their situation. "Ivana, I couldn't help but hear the conversation you were having with your mother." He looked towards Hipatia, the boys, and returned his gaze to Ivana. "I know having a child will not be easy, but I don't understand how this will keep you from being a writer? I know for certain you can be a great mother and an amazing writer." Tanner opened his arms to acknowledge everyone in the room, and said, "Everyone here will support you in any way they can."

Emilia kissed Ivana on the cheek, and said, "It's true, *mi amor.* You are going to be a great mother and a wonderful writer."

The boys rushed to their sister and hugged her. This time her tears were not from despair but from the love she felt from her family.

Tanner interrupted the moment, and said, "Ivana, I am an avid reader. I can help you with this journey. Not only will you bless this family with a child, but you will bless this world with your stories!"

Ivana's face was buried in the embrace of her family.

Tanner could barely make out the words as she

said, "Thank you."

Tanner walked back into the kitchen. He was soon followed by Emilia. She turned him around and kissed him passionately. She rested her head against his chest as they slowly rocked back and forth. "Thank you, *amor.*"

It was the first time Emilia had called him "*love.*"

Tanner's body tingled. He never wanted to let her go. She filled all the empty and painful spaces inside of him.

24

It was Christmas Day. Hipatia and Emilia were at the dining room table whispering, arguing. Emilia was waving a document in her hand.

Sebastian was in the living room with Tanner.

He played several keys on the piano; he called out the chords, "C, G, A minor, and then F."

Tanner followed the notes with the guitar. He quickened his tempo, and Sebastian jumped from his stool and clapped in approval.

"Yes! That's it!" The young boy turned his attention back to the piano, and soon the two filled the house with a beautiful melody.

Tanner closed his eyes. He smiled effortlessly as his head swayed back and forth to the rhythm of the song. Sebastian's piano playing pulled at Tanner's heart, the child was incredibly gifted. The former boxing champion was overwhelmed with emotion.

Emilia and her mother raised their voices to hear each other over the music—it was apparent that they were upset. Emilia waved the document in her mother's face. The song ended. Sebastian relaxed his shoulders, and Tanner exhaled deeply.

The beautiful moment was interrupted by Emilia shouting, "Mama, I am not going back to Ecuador! My kids are staying here! I will take them; you'll see!" She paused and turned towards her son. Emilia realized that what Sebastian had heard might upset him. She stood up from the dining room table and faced the young boy. Her eyes widened, and she said, "I love you, *mijo*."

"What's wrong, mama?" Sebastian asked, looking worried.

"*Mi amor,* please go get ready for dinner," she kissed his cheek. "Oh my God, what a beautiful song! You two should start a band!"

Sebastian chuckled, hugged his mother, and walked out of the room.

Tanner's face was still flushed as he embraced his guitar.

"What's wrong, *amor?*" she asked quietly.

Tanner shook his head, and answered, "I swear your son has been blessed by the Lord himself."

"Awe, come here," Emilia opened her arms.

Tanner hugged her tightly. He closed his eyes and kissed her.

She waited for him to open his eyes. When he did,

she said, "We need to talk."

Emilia reached for his hand. She inhaled and exhaled loudly as she guided him towards the dining room table.

Hipatia went into the kitchen to serve Christmas dinner.

Emilia slid the letter in front of Tanner, and said, "Read this." She placed her hands on her temples. Tanner reached out to touch her face. She immediately closed her eyes and started to cry.

The one-page letter was from the Department of Immigration. It was addressed to Hipatia, Emilia's mother and sponsor. It was a notice of rejection indicating that the State Department had asked Emilia and her children to leave the country by the first of February.

Tanner's hands began to shake, his face paled. "I . . . I . . . I don't understand," he stuttered.

Tanner's soul ached. It was the same feeling he'd

had when his sister lay in the hospital fighting for her life.

Emilia lifted her head; tears fell from her cheeks. "We were denied citizenship. I have to take my kids and go back to Ecuador. I don't want to leave!" She slammed a fist against the dining room table. Her beautiful, brown hair covered her face. Emilia pushed herself away from the table and turned towards the kitchen. "Mama!" she shouted.

"Amor?" her mother quietly replied.

"I'm going to clean up before dinner. I'll be right back."

Tanner remained motionless as he watched her exit the room. He turned towards Hipatia. She was sniffling as she tried to hold back her tears. Tanner felt a void inside his soul. He tried to say something to Hipatia, but she left the kitchen to comfort her daughter. He stood up from the dining table and paced nervously from the dining room to the kitchen. Tanner started talking to himself, "I love her.

I want to help her. I don't want her to leave. I love her and her children. I know it's only been a few months, but I have never been happier." Tanner chuckled nervously, "I have made dumb and reckless decisions before; what do I have to lose? At the very least, I help four loving souls find their way." He slapped his hands together as a big grin filled his face. He paused to turn on Christmas music and the house filled with the sounds of old holiday classics. Then, Tanner turned his attention to the Christmas dinner. He set the table, lit some candles, and turned off the lights to create a warm ambient glow. He was carving the turkey when Emilia raced into the kitchen.

"What are you doing, gringo?" she tried to laugh.

Tanner leaned over and kissed her cheek, "I'm carving up mama's masterpiece." He shoved a piece of turkey into his mouth, and then passed her a glass of red wine.

"Oh, you know what my grandmother used to say?" she quipped.

He laughed loudly, and responded, "No, please tell me!"

"Beware of a man who turns off the lights and offers you wine unless, of course, he is wearing an apron."

Tanner raised his glass, and said, "To grandma, may her wisdom bless this house, this family, and our marriage." He smiled widely and drank from his glass. When he was finished, he looked at Emilia.

She growled, "*What?*"

Tanner stepped backward. He turned his body to protect himself from the punch that landed on his bicep.

"What are you talking about? Did I say yes to this nonsense? No! Wait! You never bothered to even ask!" She finished her wine and raised her glass to throw it at him.

Tanner held out his hands to plead with her to stop.

"Let me finish! Please!"

Emilia paused. She lowered her glass, and said, "Go on!"

Tanner started to stutter, "W-w-well, I . . ."

"Wait," Emilia reached for the bottle and poured herself more wine. She finished the glass and started drinking from the bottle. "Okay, gringo, let's hear your story."

"When you started talking about having to leave, I felt like I was losing part of my soul. It was as if I was experiencing my mother's death all over again. I don't want you to leave. I know we've only been dating for three months, but I have never been happier."

Emilia placed the bottle on the counter and folded her arms as she nervously swayed back and forth. "Okay, *amor,* what are you thinking?" she asked.

"Well, we get married, so you and the kids can stay here. We will try to figure this out. If our marriage doesn't work, at least you and the children will be able to stay here. I love your kids, Emilia. I love you and I want to help."

Emilia whimpered, "You would do that for us?"

"Of course! Are you crazy? I'm the lucky one. I get to share this world with the most beautiful souls to ever touch my life. You will be doing me a favor!" Tanner opened his arms and approached her carefully.

"Thank you!" She kissed him. They held each other quietly.

Tanner interrupted the silence, "You know what my grandpa used to say?"

She pushed him away, and asked, "No, gringo, what?"

"If you're going to get in the water, don't just get your feet wet; jump all the way in!"

Emilia chuckled as she walked into the hallway and shouted to the kids and her mother, "Come here, my little ducklings, it's time to move the furniture; we need

room to celebrate!"

Tanner's heart raced; a new life was unfolding in front of him.

25

It was an unusually warm January day in Whisper, Oregon. Tanner was on the front porch of his place, rocking in his chair. He was dressed in navy blue slacks, a white-collared shirt, and black, leather shoes. His necktie was lying loosely across his shoulders. He took a deep breath. The smell of the forest and the ocean breeze temporarily calmed his nerves.

Tanner called his father.

"Son!" his father shouted.

Tanner chuckled nervously, "Dad, I'm sorry it's

taken so long to make this call. I promise I'll never do that again."

"Well, good deal! How are you?" his father's voice remained excited. He was breathing heavily.

Tanner shut his eyes. He could feel his father's anguish. His heart pumped against his chest, and he had a pit in his stomach. Tanner took a deep breath; his eyes remained closed, and he pressed his phone tightly against his ear. "Dad, I have never been happier in my life. I can't wait to see you and share why I'm so happy."

His father nearly lost his voice, but managed to ask, "That's great! Can you tell me why?"

"Dad, I've met someone that has filled every empty space in my soul." Tanner smiled, still rocking back and forth.

His father paused for a long moment. He stammered, "What . . . what . . . what is her name?" Where are you anyway?"

"Her name is Emilia. She is my angel. Dad, I'm also adopting her three children," Tanner was overcome with emotion. "I feel so blessed," he said humbly.

"Awe, I'm so happy for you. When can I meet her and the kids?" his father asked.

Tanner exhaled loudly, and said, "I plan on bringing the family to the farm in June after the kids are out of school. But dad, we're getting married."

"What! When? Where?" he shouted incredulously. "Aimee and I will want to be there! I know you could have your wedding on the farm! Just like your mother and I did! Wouldn't that be amazing? We could have the Reverend perform . . ."

Tanner interrupted, "Yeah, we can do that, but we're getting married today. It's a long story." Tanner said, "I like the idea of having a wedding at the farm. We'll make that happen."

"Okay! I love it! Aimee isn't here this morning,

but I'll give her the news." His father's voice was filled with joy.

"Tanner!" A call for help came from inside his apartment.

"Dad, I need to go. The boys are calling me. They're getting ready. We plan on heading to the courthouse in an hour."

"Okay, take pictures! The next time you call me, I want to hear your bride on the phone," his dad insisted.

Tanner pressed the phone even more tightly against his ear. He wanted to hug his father. "You bet, dad. I'll call you tomorrow. Love you."

"I love you, son," his dad responded.

Tanner set the phone on the arm of his rocking chair, going over the conversation he'd just had with his father.

He was soon interrupted by the sounds of laughter followed by another call for help, "Tanner!"

The former boxer, crab fisherman, and now bartender stood and exhaled loudly. He asked, "What is going on in there?" He opened the screen door, and the sound of his shoes against the wooden floor alerted the kids of his approach. The boys were in front of the vanity, trying to fasten their neckties. Omar, always the joker, grabbed one end of the tie and acted as if he was trapped in a slipknot. He made his eyes bulge and stuck out his tongue. His older brother, Sebastian, gently nudged him, and said, "You goofball!"

Sebastian continued, "We need help."

Tanner smiled widely. *This will be one of many lessons I will share with these boys*, he thought.

"Well, we're going to tie a Windsor knot—watch me," Tanner instructed.

"What is Windsor?" Omar asked curiously.

"Some dude that likes to dress up and go to fancy parties," Tanner joked.

"I want to be like Windsor!" Omar said excitedly.

Tanner chuckled, "Dear Lord." He shook his head, "How old are you?"

"Nine-and-a-half," Omar nodded approvingly.

"Okay, Gatsby Windsor, this is where we start your journey—pay attention," Tanner announced.

Tanner slowly tied the knot. The boys tried, but the big ends of the ties were closer to their chins, and the thinner ends touched their waists. They went through this exercise a few more times. After each attempt, they found that one end was somehow always longer than the other. Finally, Tanner stepped in and finished each tie for the boys.

Omar was grinning. He looked at Tanner, and asked, "Are you now our father?"

Sebastian moaned, "Omar!"

Tanner got down on one knee. He placed his hand on Omar's shoulder and waved Sebastian to step closer.

"Your father is already here. He is watching and listening," Tanner whispered and moved his head from side to side as if he was looking for their father. "I'm not sure where he is, but mark my words, he is here, and he is so proud of the both of you." He rubbed both boys on their shoulders.

Omar interrupted, "Like the noisy bird watching us from the top of a tree?"

"Yes, exactly!" Tanner looked at them. The boys were so elated to be with their new family member. "I want you both to place your hands on top of mine. I want to make a promise. I will always be here for you. I will always be here for you on your worst days and your best days. That is my promise. Let's shake on it."

The boys giggled and rushed him as they hugged him tightly.

"Come on let's go get mama, Ivana, and grandma!"

Tanner slapped their shoulders. Sebastian and Omar

followed him out of the house, mimicking Tanner's walk.

26

Emilia's eyes widened. She was nervously happy even though only her family, Tanner, and the Justice of the Peace were in the courtroom. She read her vows from a folded yellow piece of paper. "Tanner, I cannot promise the sun will rise for us in the morning, but I assure you that at this moment, my heart is filled with your love. My soul flutters with joy at first light, knowing that you are a part of our life." She pointed towards her children and her mother. Hipatia was smiling widely, her arms around Omar; Ivana held onto Sebastian. Tanner looked over at his new family. His heart raced, and his face flushed.

Emilia continued, "I promise that I will always keep your heart filled with my love. I offer you so much love that it overflows from you and touches everything that you experience. I will comfort you when you are suffering, counsel you through adversity, and encourage you throughout your journey. I will always carry you in my heart every day of every moment."

Emilia dropped her hands as tears fell from her face.

Tanner nervously grinned as he reached into his jacket and pulled out his own yellow piece of paper from the same notepad. Tanner stopped to admire Emilia. She was wearing a beautiful ivory-colored dress. Her glow radiated across the entire room. Tanner stepped a little closer. His heart continued to race as he cleared his throat.

The gray-haired, spectacled Justice of the Peace gave him a word of encouragement. "Go ahead, son," he urged.

Tanner stuttered at first—he was having trouble breathing, "Em-m-m-ilia . . . " He paused and exhaled loudly. His hands were shaking, causing Emilia to rub his fingers. Soon, Tanner was able to relax. "I have never been happier in my life. I can already feel your love inside of me. Never have I experienced so many blessings."

He looked at her and then at her children.

Emilia chortled with approval.

"I promise that I will always be here for you and your family. That my love and devotion will be unwavering. I will love your kids as if they were my own. I will be the one part of your life that you can always rely on. I will be the first to listen and the last to judge. I want to be your warmth in cold places and fresh air when you feel suffocated. I hope you are my first view every morning and my last thought every evening. I want to be your light when life seems dark and your destination when you are lost." Tanner placed the paper back in his pocket.

He looked at the kids and then into Emilia's big, brown

eyes. "I am so grateful that all of you have entered my

life. I promise to cherish these moments as a gift from

God himself."

"Good!" the Justice blurted.

After the ring ceremony, the Justice proclaimed

enthusiastically, "By the power vested in me and by the

state of Oregon, I now pronounce you husband and wife.

You may now kiss the bride."

The kids clapped and cheered as Tanner and

Emilia shared a long, passionate kiss. Omar, Sebastian,

Ivana, and Hipatia rushed the newlyweds with celebratory

shouts. They hugged each other, sharing tears and

laughter.

The Justice of the Peace tapped Tanner on the

shoulder. He leaned forward to whisper in his ear, "You

have a guest outside waiting for you."

The groom turned to face the gray-haired man, who was now smirking. He had a secret that he refused to share, Tanner thought.

Tanner raised his voice and addressed his new family, "Come on, let's go outside. Evidently, someone is waiting for us."

"Who?" Emilia asked excitedly.

Tanner shrugged. They looked at each other quizzically, and then rushed for the exit.

The sounds of giggles and heels tapping against tile echoed throughout the courthouse. When they reached the front door, they were greeted by a parade of cars decorated with balloons and graffiti. Horns blared and people shouted. Rick, their boss and owner of the Tree House, was at the bottom of the stairs with Elmer. They were grinning and tossing rice up in the air.

Tanner let out a loud laugh and started clapping. When they reached the bottom of the stairs, Rick gave

Emilia a hug and shook Tanner's hand. Elmer embraced both. Rick shouted over the sound of the horns.

"We're throwing a private party at the Tree House for all of you. Drinks and food are on the house. I hope you don't mind; we have invited a few people." Rick and Elmer laughed.

Tanner looked at the mile-long parade of cars, and asked jokingly, "Is anyone not invited?"

Rick chuckled and slapped him on the back, and said, "The parade awaits the guests of honor—lead the way!"

Hipatia clutched Rick and hugged him tightly. She laughed, kissed him, and thanked him repeatedly. Then, the family made their way to Hipatia's Suburban. The car was decorated with balloons and window markers with the words *Just Married* on every side of the vehicle. Omar and Sebastian giggled as they ran towards the car.

Hipatia drove to the front of the procession.

Everyone was waving and honking their horns as she slowly headed towards the tavern.

When they entered the tavern, they were greeted by a band playing an old Spanish song—*Kumbala*.

Emilia grabbed Tanner's hand and led him to the dance floor. A long table was set up at one end filled with a wide variety of foods and desserts. It was a massive potluck that had been cleverly kept a secret but was now revealed in a gesture of great generosity.

A warm, bountiful energy, rarely felt in this sleepy town, occupied every soul inside the Tree House. Tanner and Emilia soaked in their moment. They held each other's gaze while the sounds of music, laughter, and celebratory dancing surrounded them. It had only taken three months for them to go from throwing shot glasses and insults at each other to feeling a deep, intimate connection that many people rarely experience.

They held each other tightly. Tanner felt Emilia's

heartbeat as her warm, sweet breath exhaled against his neck.

He closed his eyes and whispered into her ear, "I never want this to end."

27

Kenny pulled his old pickup into the Harris Hospital parking garage in Dallas. Aimee was fidgeting with her fingernails.

Kenny looked over at her and asked, "Are you nervous, honey?"

She shook her head. She signed, "Overwhelmed."

Kenny reached for her hand and squeezed gently. He gave her a warm smile of encouragement.

Aimee rubbed the top of her father's hand. She took a deep breath, released her hand from her father's grasp, and opened the truck door.

They were soon in the hospital lobby waiting for the surgical team to take Aimee to pre-op to prepare her for surgery. She was on her phone.

Kenny leaned over to peek at her phone. "What are you looking at, honey?"

Aimee turned her phone towards her father. She was looking at land for sale in West Texas.

"What's this—do you want to buy . . . ?"

"Aimee Childress," a nurse called from the entrance to the surgical ward. She held a clipboard in her hand.

Aimee stood from her chair and faced her father. She made a fist with each hand and crossed her arms against her chest and signed "I love you."

"I love you, too. Just think, the next time we see each other, you can tell me that in your own voice."

That made her smile. She blew him a kiss, then

followed the nurse into the surgical ward.

Kenny wandered around the hospital lobby and found a newspaper and coffee. The morning had passed when Aimee's physician found Kenny in the waiting room.

"Kenny Childress?"

Kenny hurriedly folded the newspaper and stood to greet the doctor.

"Yes, that's me. How is Aimee?"

"She is fine. The surgery was a success. She is resting now."

Kenny slapped his hands loudly.

"I have more good news for you, Mr. Childress."

"Okay, doc, or should I call you Santa?"

The doctor chuckled. "We have a new grant program. We want to keep your daughter here for three weeks for intensive speech therapy. When she leaves the hospital, she will be talking more than a pet parrot."

"Sign us up!"

"Okay, we'll get started and Aimee will be ready to go home in three weeks."

28

"I hate being on the farm alone. Thank you for staying with me the last three weeks," Kenny said to Stacey.

They were having breakfast at the farmhouse.

Kenny looked at his watch and then stood up in a hurry. He drank out of his coffee mug while putting his empty plate in the sink.

Stacey managed to stand in front of him. She held onto his arm and placed her palm against his stomach. "I got this. Go get Aimee." She kissed him on the lips.

Kenny's eyes were closed. She gave him goose bumps. He shook himself to clear his head.

Then, he shouted as he raced for the door, "See you tomorrow!"

After the seven-hour drive to the hospital, Kenny parked in the garage, and raced into the lobby. His daughter was sitting in a comfortable leather chair, looking at her phone.

He was ten feet away but paused and asked softly, "Aimee?"

Aimee looked up from her phone. She was beaming. She placed her phone in her purse, stood up, and walked towards her dad. Her face became flushed as tears fell from her cheeks.

"Papa, I'm here, and I love you."

Kenny grabbed his daughter and held her tightly. They laughed, jumped, and howled.

"Let's go home!" Kenny shouted.

They ran towards the exit, laughing the entire way.

Aimee started talking once they were in the pickup truck and continued on the freeway heading home.

"Dad, I have so much to tell you."

"Awesome, tell me everything, honey."

"Dad, I want to build a small school for battered children. I want to find land close to the farm. I still have a lot of classes to finish my degree, but I want to put so much detail into this schoolhouse. I want it to be a boarding school—a haven for these children. Everything from books, playground, dining, the art, I want all of these things and more to help foster these kids and to help develop them with their growth."

"What a wonderful idea. It will give you a great sense of purpose. You have all my support."

"Will you help me find a property close to the farm? I want to live at the farmhouse—I want to look for approximately forty acres, with . . . "

Every word Aimee spoke filled his heart.

29

Two months later.

Tanner and Emilia were walking barefoot on the beach, holding hands. It was early March. A cool ocean breeze kept the temperature close to seventy degrees. The wet sand from last night's rain pressed between their toes as they continued their late afternoon walk.

Emilia broke the silence, "So, you want to move to Texas?"

Tanner squeezed her hand and nodded.

"What about the forest, the ocean, this beach, our

friends, the kids' friends? Won't we miss all of it? I know I will miss the beach and the forest," Emilia confessed.

She released his hand and bent over to pick up a small, smooth rock shaped like a heart. She held it in her hand and placed it in her pocket. Emilia trusted Tanner but was not fond of the heat or being away from this beautiful place. Emilia hesitated as she tried to make a decision.

"The family farm is an amazing place for children. They can watch and learn how to nurture animals and crops. It is a special feeling to witness a harvest from seed to fruit or watch the birth of a baby foal. They will never receive an education quite like the one a child learns on a farm," Tanner argued.

Emilia turned and looked into Tanner's eyes. She loved how he thought of her kids first. She kissed him. "Tell me more," Emilia said.

Tanner sensed she was beginning to warm up to the idea. He raised his voice in excitement. They continued to walk along the shore.

Emilia dropped her head to listen intently to her husband's words.

"Well, Ivana will have you, her grandmother, and my dad, my sister, me, to help with the baby. My father knows the dean of a private university that recruits young, aspiring authors. She will be so happy! We can build Sebastian a studio so he can compose and record music. The house is big enough for all of us, but we can build a small place for your mom. Omar . . ." Tanner laughed. The boy was so easy to please. "There are plenty of places to fish. We can fish, fish, fish," Tanner added.

Emilia turned to Tanner with a concerned look. "What about me?" she asked.

"Well, I'm not sure what you want to do? Do you want to go to school? Find a different career? Be a stay-at-home mom? It's up to you, whatever you want to do, angel."

Emilia was deep in thought. He made it sound so perfect. She stared down at the sand and nodded hesitantly. "It sounds wonderful, *mi amor*. How about we visit your papa and sister this summer and decide then? We need to discuss this with the kids and with my mother too."

Tanner agreed. They walked a little farther before turning back towards the car.

They pulled up at Hipatia's house. The fresh sea air and the warmth from burning cedar in the fireplace always welcomed Emilia home. She loved her mother. Being close to her mom reminded her of simpler times in her life. Emilia had grown up on a family farm in Ecuador with her grandmother and mother. That memory softened the idea of moving to Texas. Working as a waitress in a bar was spiritually unfulfilling. Her family filled her soul, but she had begun to think about improving her work experience and her life. "I think it's time to make a change. Even if we decide to stay here," she concluded privately.

Hipatia shouted from the kitchen, "Dinner is ready!"

The kids appeared from their bedrooms and made their way to the dining room. Emilia and Tanner were met by Hipatia's warm smile as she placed *empanadas* on the table.

"Well, how are my lovebirds?" she laughed.

"We are fine, mama."

Emilia took a deep breath. The kids sensed that something was bothering their mother.

Omar stood up from the kitchen table and raced to his mama and hugged her. She squeezed him tightly and Emilia started to giggle. She brushed her son's hair away from his face and kissed him on the forehead.

"Oh, my sweet boy," she whispered to him.

The table was filled with so many blessings—the

ceviche, empanadas, the stories, and the family.

When they'd finished eating most of their dinner, Emilia started, "What do you think about us moving to a farm in Texas with Tanner's family."

Sebastian shouted, "Yes!"

Hipatia laughed with joy and nodded, *"Si, creo que es una gran idea!* (Yes, I think it's a great idea.)"

Ivana, who was starting to show, moaned, "Yes, please. I want to leave Whisper."

Omar, who was sitting next to Tanner, looked worried, "What about fishing? I want to fish."

Tanner leaned over towards the young boy, smiled, and asked, "How about we make our own lake?" He nudged at his elbow and then opened his arms, "We can design our very own lake!"

Omar bounced in his seat. He was excited. "What would we call the lake?"

Tanner looked into Omar's eyes for a moment and

felt filled with love. He wanted to honor him.

It was as if the Universe whispered into his ear.

"Let's call it *Guevara's Landing.*"

Omar chuckled, looked up at the ceiling, and shouted, "Yes, perfect!"

Tanner turned to Emilia. She was smiling, her heart nearly jumping out of her body. She nodded and whispered to Tanner, "Okay, we will do this."

Omar interrupted, "When! When can we go?"

Tanner rubbed Omar's head and then turned to face the entire table. "When you are finished with school, we'll go out there and have a look. We can talk about moving to Texas after we visit the farm."

They all replied, "Yes!"

"Oh, somebody's birthday is on June 2!" Tanner announced. "So, we have to wait until after that very important birthday before we leave!" He raised his index finger in the air as if he was making an important point.

The kids laughed. Emilia's birthday was coming up, and they were already secretly planning her party.

30

Aimee and Stacey were in the kitchen laughing over a story that she shared about her brother when they were both toddlers. It was a tale Aimee's father had told repeatedly over the years. Aimee's voice rose as she continued laughing. "He put his hands inside the BBQ and grabbed a handful of coal and ash, then decided to paint both our faces. After we were done running around the house screaming and chasing our dogs, Tanner thought it was best to clean up before mom found us dirty, so he snuck into the kitchen thinking he would get the soap, but he grabbed a bottle of bleach instead."

A knock on the door interrupted Aimee's story.

Kenny announced from the bedroom, "I got it. It's Hugh. He wanted to drop by and talk with me."

"Who is Hugh?" Stacey asked.

"He has the small farm just east of the orchard. Hugh has lived there all his life; he must be close to eighty years old."

Then Kenny turned and opened the front door.

"Hugh! Come on in. It's so nice to see you. How have you been? How is Vivian?" Kenny greeted his old friend.

Hugh was a hardworking farmer. He always wore a pair of slightly stained overalls. His skin was coarse from years of working in the sun. He took his hat off his head and Kenny motioned for him to have a seat on the sofa.

"Vivian is not doing well, Kenny. She has Alzheimer's and I couldn't take care of her anymore. I placed her in a home several weeks ago," His voice was scratchy from years of smoking several packs of cigarettes a day.

"I'm so sorry, Hugh. Do you need us to help with anything?"

"Well," he exhaled, and said, "no, thank you, but I'm putting the farm up for sale, and I thought I would give you the courtesy of making the first offer."

Aimee was listening in the kitchen. She rushed into the living room.

Hugh turned his gaze towards Aimee. He smiled. "Hello, Aimee—I never get tired of seeing your children grown, Kenny."

"Awe, thank you, Hugh," Aimee replied.

Hugh leaned back on the couch looking stunned.

"I wasn't expecting that! I'm at a loss for words. Kenny, you've been holding out on me. Aimee can talk again!"

Stacey entered the living room with two glasses of
freshly squeezed lemonade and handed Hugh a glass.

"Here you go, Hugh," Stacey smiled. "My name is
Stacey."

Hugh's mouth dropped open. He looked at Kenny
and said jokingly, "Instead of looking at the stars at night
with my telescope, I should have aimed it at the Childress
farm."

Kenny and Hugh both let out a long belly laugh.

Aimee interrupted, "Hugh, I want to buy the farm.
Let me know how much you want for it."

Hugh smiled at Aimee and nodded, "Will do,
Aimee. It's yours."

31

Three months later.

Omar rested his ear against Ivana's stomach. She was now seven months pregnant.

Ivana let out a loud burp! "Oh my, the little monster is an eater," she joked.

Ivana rubbed her brother's hair. Omar looked up at her and giggled.

"Sorry, Marcito, he loves to eat." She let out another burp! "Oh! *Mi Dios!*" Ivana reached for her carbonated water and took another long sip through a straw. "Be careful, *amor*; my monster can get a little gassy!"

Omar playfully screamed. He pulled his head away from his sister's stomach.

She shrugged, "Well, he can't help it."

Ivana leaned to her left, squinted, and lifted her leg.

Omar screamed, "Ivana!"

Sebastian and Emilia watched from the dining room. Their laughter interrupted the siblings' banter.

Tanner heard them from the bedroom. He was nearly finished making the bed when Emilia's salsa music ringtone signaled her to retrieve her phone from the nightstand.

It was Emilia's birthday. The children were in high spirits. They were preparing for mama's birthday party. Ivana had purposely scheduled an appointment with her doctor, so she could get her mother out of the house.

Emilia danced and sang towards her phone. She answered, "Well, hello, Papa Kenny!"

Tanner smiled so widely that all his teeth were showing. Emilia winked at him.

"Happy birthday to you! Happy birthday . . ." Emilia pressed the speakerphone and covered her mouth.

Kenny continued, "Happy birthday, dear Emilia! Happy birthday to you!"

"Awe, thank you, Papa!" It made her heart happy to call him "Papa."

"What is my favorite daughter-in-law doing for her birthday?" he asked.

Emilia laughed, "I am your only daughter-in-law! Well, I don't know. . . What are we doing, Tanner?"

Tanner returned the pillows to the bed. He straightened, and said, "Well, I thought I'd spoil her with sweet kisses and dancing."

"Hah! That's your birthday present, son?"

Emilia echoed, "Yeah, Tanner! That's your birthday present?"

Tanner gave her a sheepish grin but remained silent.

"We can't wait to see you and Aimee! We'll be there next week!" she said excitedly.

"Oh, I know. We are so excited to meet you and your kids," he replied.

"Mama, we need to go! My angel has a doctor's appointment," Ivana shouted from the living room.

"Papa Kenny, I need to go. Ivana has a checkup with the doctor. Thank you, for calling."

"You bet, Emilia. Tanner, I can't wait to see you too! I love you, son."

"See you soon, Dad. Love you too!"

Emilia walked into Tanner's open arms. They held each other tightly and started to kiss. That was all Tanner needed. He moved her towards the bed, but she wrestled away from his arms and laughed loudly. "What are you thinking, gringo? I have to take your daughter to the doctor!" she mused.

As soon as Ivana and Emilia were in the car, Hipatia raced towards the kitchen. She shouted to the boys to follow. Tanner reached for his cell phone.

"Hello, Rick, yeah, she left. Bring the city over; we will throw her a birthday party she will never forget," Tanner chuckled.

Within thirty minutes, the first knock echoed through the house. It was Elmer. He was wearing a kilt.

Tanner shouted, "Yeah! Now, this party can get started!"

Elmer held a case of champagne. He noticed Hipatia in the kitchen. "Excuse me, son," he winked, handed Tanner the champagne, and headed towards Tanner's mother-in-law.

A few minutes later, Rick arrived with his crew,

who brought in folding chairs, tables, and arms full of food. Sebastian was so excited. He sat at the piano and serenaded everyone throughout the house.

Each visitor entered the Guevara home, giving hugs and sharing smiles.

Soon the band, La Revancha, arrived.

Cars spilled out on the driveway and down the street. Tanner and Emilia had become Whisper's pride and joy. The former boxing champion and the Ecuadorian queen had stolen the hearts of the villagers.

Ivana had finished her checkup and convinced her mom to take her shopping for baby clothes. Not that Emilia needed much convincing.

Tanner stood in one corner of the backyard holding a cold beer. Elmer walked up to his self-proclaimed adopted son. He would often repeat how he had met Tanner on a bench at the city center park. "Well . . . " Elmer smiled as he approached Tanner, and asked, "what do you think, son?"

"Elmer, I'm at a loss for words. All of you have touched my soul," Tanner confided.

The old man rubbed his shoulder and smiled. He turned and faced the party with Tanner,

"Oh, that reminds me," Elmer reached for his cell that was secured inside his high socks.

He quickly texted. "I need to let Ivana know we are ready to get this party started."

Tanner took a drink from his beer. All he could do was nod and smile.

The band started. They were a fixture in town. The three-man ensemble could play any song in every popular genre. Rick rushed over to Elmer and Tanner.

"Hey bud—there are three characters from Washington at the door who say they know you."

Tanner shouted, "Douglas, AJ, and Ignacio! Yes!"

He hurried towards the front of the house. When

he finally made it to the front door, he was met with shouts and hugs. Douglas, AJ, and Ignacio sported tans. Ignacio had brought his wife, Paki.

"I can't believe you are all here!" Tanner said happily.

AJ joked, "Yeah, we left margaritas and the beach for this. Why we spent all those years in that stinky vessel hunting big bugs is a mystery!"

"Where is that lovely bride of yours?" Ignacio interrupted. "We want to meet your Ecuadorian queen. Tanner, I brought my Ecuadorian queen, Paki."

They hugged.

She spoke to him in Spanish, *"Hola, es un placer conocerte finalmente.* (Hello, it's a pleasure to finally meet you.)"

"Emilia should be here any minute. My daughter . . ." Tanner explained.

"Oh, your daughter!" Ignacio grinned.

"Yes, my daughter is at the doctor for a checkup. She is seven months pregnant," he boasted.

His three friends surrounded Tanner, slapping his shoulders. Tanner took another sip from his beer and smiled widely.

Ivana turned onto the street where her grandmother lived. There were cars parked down the entire block. She asked quizzically, "What is this? What is going on, mama?"

Emilia chuckled, "I wonder, *mija.*" Emilia loved a good party—one that touched your heart—compelling you to dance and sing underneath the stars. Her soul was floating off the ground.

"Hoo hoo hoo!" she hung out the passenger window, pumping her arms up in the air. As soon as Ivana stopped the car, Emilia opened the door and raced up the driveway. Ivana laughed loudly. She loved seeing her mother so happy.

Emilia stopped to hug each guest. Someone handed her a glass of wine. The sound of La Revancha filled the street. She started to dance with every passerby.

Rick tapped Tanner on the shoulder. Elmer was at the window laughing at something going on in the front yard. Tanner waved the *Obrien* crew over to the front window. It was his bride dancing excitedly in the front yard, a glass of wine in her hand. Ignacio lost his breath and held his heart,

"That is Emilia?" he asked.

"Yes, she's the one that stole my heart," Tanner shared.

Paki whispered, *"Es tan hermosa. (She is so beautiful)"*

"Thank you, Paki," Tanner replied. "Excuse me for just one moment."

Tanner walked out the front door and stood on the front steps. Emilia was moving her hips to the rhythm of the song, singing, with her glass of wine raised over her head. His bride was surrounded by partygoers. She had the entire front yard of guests dancing.

Tanner made his way towards the birthday girl. The circle surrounding her opened for him. She lifted her head and noticed her husband. She handed her glass of wine to one of the guests and jumped into his arms. They laughed, kissed, and danced.

Emilia whispered in his ear, "Thank you for everything. I love you so much."

Tanner squeezed her, and said, "I never want to let you go."

They were interrupted by an announcement from Leo, La Revancha's lead singer, "I hear the guest of honor is here."

This was followed by screams.

"Where is my singer? Where is Emilia?" Leo called.

The band started to play *Bésame Mucho*. Emilia screamed with excitement and made her way through the house and into the backyard.

She sang off-key, but no one cared. Rick handed her a bottle of wine. She waved the band to continue as she drank from the bottle. Emilia raised her arms above her head.

Everyone in the backyard started dancing and singing along, "*Bésame Mucho!*"

The night arrived, and the birthday party continued. Emilia and Paki were huddled in a corner, reminiscing about Ecuador. The *Obrien* crew, Rick, and Elmer were on the front porch teasing Tanner.

"So, Tanner, thank God that Emilia has poor eyesight and a soft heart for rescues."

They laughed.

Emilia walked out to the front porch with her mama.

"What's going on out here?" She placed her arms around Tanner. *"Mi amor,* we are out of toilet paper. Mama and I are going to the store; we'll be right back."

"Let me go, baby. It's your birthday," Tanner offered.

"No, you've been drinking, and you are with your friends. Mama is sober; she can drive. You know what my grandma says?"

Tanner rolled his eyes, smiled, and shook his head from side to side, and said, "I can only imagine."

Emilia punched his shoulder, "Don't make fun of my grandma; she is my world."

Tanner turned to face the group. He was holding his laughter. "Ok, what does your grandma say?"

"Don't let your guests reach for the good towels; you will need them to wipe up the spilled wine."

Everyone laughed.

Emilia kissed him, and Hipatia kissed his cheek.

He watched them both leave.

Emilia put her arm around her mother as they sang towards her car.

Elmer stared at Tanner. The look on his face reminded Elmer of how he used to look at his Sophie.

Rick burped loudly and then asked, "Who needs a beer?"

They all laughed and followed him into the backyard for another beer. The band continued to play into the night as Rick made sure the three had beers. Leo had started slurring his words, but no one cared.

An hour passed. Ignacio approached Tanner. His eyes were wide, and his face was pale.

"Tanner, you need to go to the front door."

The expression on Ignacio's face caused Tanner's throat to tighten. He tried to speak, but instinct told him to race to the door.

He was greeted by Sheriff Reeder.

Tanner looked concerned, "What's going on, TJ?"

The sheriff held his hat in his hand. He looked down and began to stutter, trying to breathe.

Tanner stepped forward, and asked, "What is it!"

"Tanner, there has been an accident." TJ's face filled with tears.

"No!" he cried.

"Emilia and Hipatia were hit head-on by a logging truck. I'm . . . I'm sorry, Tanner."

"Where are they? Are they at the hospital?"

TJ convulsed as he spoke, "They're gone, Tanner."

Tanner fell to his knees. He could only hear his breathing. Holding his stomach, he started to vomit. Then Tanner repeatedly cried, "No! No! No! Oh God!" He vomited again.

Ignacio stood behind him silently. Elmer was on the front porch, weeping. AJ and Douglas had their arms around each other, praying loudly. Everyone stood in disbelief.

Tanner picked himself up and stumbled into the forest. He purposely found a thorny manzanita bush and lay against it; hoping the brush would transfer his pain from his heart to his body.

He was dry heaving. After a few minutes, he started to dismantle the manzanita bush. His hands were bloodied.

The band had stopped playing. Headlights pierced into the night as the party emptied.

Tanner rubbed his hands on the forest floor and pulled at the underbrush. Then, in shock, a voice filled his head, "The kids." Tanner cried again, "The kids," and he ran towards the house.

The kids were huddled in a circle against the wall in the living room. Paki stood close by, trying to console them. Paki noticed Tanner approaching and stepped away from the children.

"Come with me. We are going to the bedroom," Tanner demanded.

The children held their stomachs and tears filled their faces.

Ignacio called from the living room, "Can I help, Tanner?"

"Get everyone out of here!" he replied.

The children sat on the edge of the bed. Omar and Sebastian rested their heads against Ivana's shoulders.

Tanner went down to his knees in front of the kids, tears fell from his face.

After about thirty minutes, Tanner spoke to the children, "I want you all to sleep in this bed together. I don't want any of you to separate from each other."

Ivana whimpered, "What about you? Where will you sleep?"

"On the floor, next to you. I want you to lay down and hold onto each other. I'm going to turn off the lights.

You won't sleep, but it's important that you comfort each other."

Tanner turned off the lights and lit a few candles. He could barely breathe. The children cried throughout the night while Tanner sat in a chair and wept for his bride.

The following day, they tried to watch a movie, but Omar broke out in tears, then Ivana and Sebastian. There was an occasional knock on the door. Someone would drop food off for the family. It would just sit in the kitchen and rot. No one had an appetite.

For nearly a week, the sounds of tears or the cries from nightmares filled Tanner and Emilia's bedroom.

32

"Tanner?" Ivana quietly called from the other side of his bedroom door.

He was staring at the ceiling fan. His hands clutched his chest tightly. It had been seven days since Emilia and Hipatia had passed away. Tanner wiped the tears from his eyes and called out to Ivana, "Give me a minute, sweetheart." He jumped from the bed and rushed to the bathroom. He wiped his face with a warm, wet cloth and relaxed by taking a few long, slow, deep breaths.

"I need to be strong for the kids," he uttered. He

shook his head from side to side and stretched his arms.

Tanner cleared his throat. "Coming!" he shouted.

When he opened the bedroom door, he was greeted by a hug from Ivana. She buried her head in his chest and cried. Tanner rocked her back and forth. He kept himself from crying.

He whispered, "Come on in, let's watch a movie; I'll get your brothers."

She nodded and tried to breathe through her nose but could only manage to exhale loudly.

Ivana noticed the bed was made. She crossed her arms, and asked, "Tanner, have you slept?"

He lied, "Yes, I just slept on top of the bed. I felt restless, that's all."

She nodded again.

Tanner called out from the bedroom, "Marcito, Sebastian?"

The boys quickly entered the hallway from their

bedroom with headphones resting on their necks.

"Come here, boys; let's watch a movie."

Omar reached Tanner first and hugged him tightly, then held out his other arm for Sebastian. He held onto them tightly.

Tanner released the boys and stood up straight.

He handed his credit card to Sebastian, and said, "Order us some food. Whatever you want."

Sebastian took the card and hurried towards his sister, who was sitting on the bed rubbing her very pregnant stomach. Her brother tried to comfort her. "What do Ivanita and my little nephew want to eat? What do you say, Little One?" he asked, talking to her baby.

"Order a bunch of pizzas," she answered and rubbed her stomach.

"Okay," her brother replied, adding "what do you want on them?"

"Lots of toppings," Ivana continued to rub her fat

belly. "And dessert, I might need dessert," she burped.

It was the first time the kids had been truly hungry. They'd only picked at their food the past week.

The thought of eating caused Ivana to close her mouth and swallow her saliva. She wiped the side of her lips and rocked.

"Order some of those jalapeno and cream cheese poppers too!"

Sebastian laughed, "You got it, *gorda!*"

Tanner handed Omar the remote, and said, "Pick something out, Marcito."

Ivana whined, "No, Omar. Please, not a bang-bang movie."

Tanner chuckled, "You all figure it out." He left the room and walked out the front door.

He breathed in the cool ocean air. It was early afternoon. Every time he looked at her children, he was reminded of Emilia.

"I am the only family they have now," Tanner said softly. He kneeled down, picked up a handful of dirt and dead pine needles, and rubbed them between his hands. Tanner looked up at the top of the trees at the light blue sky smattered with white, puffy clouds. He lowered his head as a gust of wind pushed him from his stance. Still clutching the pine needles and dirt in his hands, he said aloud, "I am angry, God." He tossed the dirt and needles to the ground, wiped his hands against his jeans, and stepped back into the house. Tanner walked into the bedroom and discovered that all three kids were holding onto each other under the covers.

"Just in time, Tanner. The movie is about to start."

Tanner grabbed the only chair in the bedroom. He sat quietly and watched the movie, occasionally looking over from time to time at the kids. He admired how much they loved and cared for each other. *Emilia was a great mother*, he thought.

The food soon arrived. The kids gorged on it, littering pizza boxes, napkins, and paper plates on the bed. After eating, they all fell fast asleep. Tanner chuckled, paused the movie, and picked up the trash.

He quietly shut the door, grabbed the keys to Emily's car and headed to Elmer's place.

Elmer was on the front porch. He was drinking scotch early today. He waved as Tanner entered the driveway.

Elmer rocked on his rocking chair, and remarked, "Son, what a nice surprise."

Tanner leaned over and shook Elmer's free hand. He sat on a porch swing near his friend. Elmer looked at his glass while fingering the ice. Finally, he took a sip and chewed on an ice cube.

The old man cleared his throat, and spoke, "I often think of my Sophie. She was so loving. Sometimes, I would bring my stress from work—paying bills, raising children, whatever—and I would say something rotten to her."

Elmer shook his head and took a long drink.

He looked down at his glass, and confessed, "No matter how dark the demons that occupied my head were, she would shine her loving light right into my heart. Every night, by the end of the day, I was grateful to be in her arms."

Tanner began to swing; he leaned forward, staring at his feet, his hands clutching the swing's chain. "Yeah, well, God apparently doesn't want me to experience that."

Elmer sighed loudly and got up from his chair. The older man returned with two fresh glasses filled with ice and a newly opened bottle. He handed one of the glasses to Tanner and filled it with scotch.

Elmer waited for Tanner to finish his first glass and then poured him another.

The old man started, "Is this the same God who

created life on a spinning rock hovered in space filled with billions of other spinning planets and stars? A universal accident? I don't think so. The same God that births the flowers in the spring? The one that inspires the migration of the butterflies, created sanctuaries for the ladybugs, and orchestrated the journey of the humpback whales? That God—the one that brings light into my heart every morning? The creator of the glorious human design that brings me to tears by witnessing the sweetest sincere act of kindness? That God?"

Tanner stopped swinging, sat up, and forced a smile. He could feel warm energy begin to enter his body.

Elmer set his drink down, leaned towards the young man, and continued, "The same God that has empowered you to be in her children's lives. Who knows? What is the significance of Ivana's child? What is your role? How will we know?" Elmer rocked quietly for a moment. A painful memory surfaced. He picked up his drink and tears fell from his eyes. "That war, that awful war, so much destruction, and so much death." Elmer paused momentarily and caught his breath.

"That destruction was not from the glory of God. That was from the hearts of evil men. God had nothing to do with it."

Elmer pointed his finger at Tanner, and said, "It was from the purest hearts that we were saved from darkness—men and women who felt and lived God's creation that saved humanity."

Tanner smiled, "I think I understand what you are trying to say." He set his glass down and began to sway, looking out into the forest.

Tanner lowered his voice and said profoundly, "Emilia and Hipatia's accident may have been just an accident or maybe it was a fateful decision decreed by our Creator. If it was simply an accident, it was the manifestation of an act that happened among an infinite number of simultaneous actions. They simply collided, and their bodies were destroyed, but their souls continue to live."

"Yes, Tanner!"

Elmer stood up and refreshed both of their drinks. He then held out his glass and they toasted, "To Emilia! The brightest stars always burn the fastest!"

Tanner looked up and laughed as tears fell down his cheeks.

"Make no mistake. Your Emilia will always live inside you," Elmer counseled.

"What about the evil acts? The wars? Why doesn't God do something about them?" Tanner asked.

Elmer smiled, "That is a great question. I've spent most of my life asking that same question. It turns out that I already had the answer. When we are born, is it a natural thought to harbor evil? Do we scheme for power? Do we seek to control?"

"No," Tanner replied, "we seek understanding, love, nourishment, and acceptance, among other needs."

"Exactly, now imagine *not* understanding the glory of our Creator's design or experiencing the power of universal love. I believe God intended us to nurture and nourish his people. Part of that nurturing is to educate and share with others that we are all included in this great miracle." Elmer replied. He shook his glass, and continued, "Well, even though we were created in the most divinely beautiful design, most humans decide to ask ungrateful questions such as: What's in it for me? or why did this happen to me?" Elmer shook his head and rocked back in his chair.

A long pause ensued.

Tanner finally disrupted the silence by asking, "What questions should we ask?"

"Don't ask me, Tanner. Ask God," Elmer replied.

Tanner and Elmer sat quietly on the porch for the

remainder of the afternoon. Tanner was comforted by the sun while the ocean breeze dried his tears. The rhythmic sound of Elmer's squeaking rocking chair kept Tanner in deep thought.

Elmer remained silent.

Tanner finished his drink and stood up from the porch swing. "I need to take the kids to the farm. A change of scenery will help us heal," he said with resolve.

Elmer stopped rocking and pressed his hand against his heart. "That's the spirit, Tanner!"

"My family will fill those tender young hearts with love. The harvest will give them a front seat to one of God's miracles, and there are very few experiences quite like a friendship with a horse."

Elmer laughed joyfully.

"I'll watch Hipatia's place. Get out of here today! Leave the house keys on the kitchen counter. I will pick them up tomorrow morning," he offered.

"Awesome! Thank you!" Tanner rushed to the old man and squeezed him tightly.

Elmer laughed while slapping Tanner's back.

Tanner stepped back, and said, "Elmer Keith, it is no coincidence that you and I crossed paths."

"No, it's not, son. You see, that park bench was the place Sophie and I visited routinely. I hadn't been there since she passed away. When a pigeon landed on my porch that morning, I was reminded of the park. I was so overcome with emotion that I went to feed the birds that morning," he confessed. "Then you arrived," Elmer smiled.

Tanner beamed. He started down the stairs and shouted, "See you in the fall!" he replied.

"I'll see you when I see you!" Elmer retorted.

Tanner rushed back to the house. The kids were listening to music on the porch. They stopped and waved as he pulled into the driveway.

Ivana shouted, "Where have you been, Poopie?"

Tanner quickly exited the car and paused.

Apparently, he'd earned a new nickname.

He chuckled loudly, "Poopie? Okay."

They all replied, "Yes, Poopie!"

"Well, Poopie wants to know if you all want to go to Texas?" Tanner grinned.

"Yes!" the kids cheered.

"Okay, the last one packed sits in the middle," Tanner announced.

They ran into the house and raced to their bedrooms.

Nearly an hour had passed. Finally, everyone was ready, except for Ivana. She sat on the edge of her bed calling out what she needed the boys to pack for her. "No, not that color. The yellow blouse," she commanded.

Omar groaned, "Come on, Ivana!"

Sebastian and Tanner chuckled.

Tanner grabbed the boys' suitcases and headed towards the car. He started the SUV and purposely stepped on the gas to alert the kids that he was ready to leave.

Tanner heard Ivana shout, "Remember what my mother would say, if you are in a hurry, don't bother packing the donkey!"

Omar laughed, "Mama never said that!"

"Well, she just did, *mijo*," she said smugly.

A few minutes later, Sebastian, Ivana, and Omar walked out the front door. Sebastian and Omar were holding their sister's bags.

Tanner placed the luggage in the back of Hipatia's SUV. "I have good news, Poopies!" Tanner replied.

The kids stopped and listened anxiously. He grinned, "There is no middle seat!"

The kids cheered and piled into the car.

Tanner backed down the driveway and headed

East. He'd left the house open with the keys on the

kitchen counter for Elmer.

He thought to himself, "I have everything of value with

me—these kids and our memories."

33

Tanner drove through California, and they were just crossing into Nevada. Sebastian and Omar played games on their phones, and Ivana's eyes were closed. She'd placed a pillow against the passenger window and leaned against it. Ivana kept her hands on her stomach. She cried quietly occasionally as she continued to mourn the loss of her mother and grandmother.

Tanner broke the silence by asking, "Is anyone hungry?"

They all replied in chorus, "Yes."

He pulled off the freeway and into a large truck stop with an enormous skillet the size of a bus mounted on the top of its roof. There were semi-trucks of all shapes and colors moving in and out of the parking lot. Tanner found a place to park and they were greeted by a young girl holding two white, curly-haired fox terrier puppies in her arms.

Ivana admired the pups, and said, "They are so precious."

The young girl responded, "I'm selling these cuties for fifty dollars each."

Tanner walked around the vehicle and looked at the kids. They had crowded around the girl. Ivana had taken one of the puppies in her arms and was being accosted by kisses and licks on her cheek, which made her giggle.

Tanner handed the girl fifty dollars. Omar rushed towards Tanner and hugged him. The Texan squeezed tightly and exhaled. The kids took turns kissing the puppy.

"What will we call her?" Sebastian asked, scratching the little terrier's head.

He watched the kids enjoy the new member of the family and then finally said, "Let's go to a drive-through so we can have our first meal with Girl Dog."

Ivana frowned disapprovingly, and said, "That's not her name!" She held the fox terrier close to her face as the puppy continued to lick and give her kisses.

They all hurried into the car, and Tanner found a drive-thru hamburger place a few blocks from the truck stop. They ordered their food and continued traveling towards Texas.

Ivana was feeding the puppy a piece of her hamburger. She kissed the top of her white, curly-haired head. "What is your name, cutie?" The puppy gulped its food and began licking her hand.

With a mouth full of hamburger, Omar replied,

"What about Woona?"

"What, Woona? No, Gordo, I don't like it," Ivana responded.

Omar swallowed his food and took a sip of his drink to clear his throat.

"No, I said Moona. She is the color of a full moon, and it's a Spanglish name."

Ivana lifted the white fox terrier to her face and whispered, "Do you like Moona?"

The puppy wagged its tail, barked, and licked Ivana's cheek.

"Okay, Moona, it is!" She turned to hand the puppy to Omar, "Please take Moona, Marcito; I want to finish my food."

Sebastian reached out and rubbed the puppy's head, and said, "Welcome, to the family, Moona Guevara!"

Ivana turned to Tanner, and said, "Tell us more

about your family and the farm."

Tanner gripped the wheel as he paused to think about how to respond. So much had happened in his life. "Well, I lost my mother when I was young. She was a beautiful soul. She liked to sing to my sister Aimee and me," Tanner choked up, "I think about her often,"

"Awe, I bet." Ivana took a sip of her drink and burped playfully.

"Oops, sorry," she giggled, "my child likes to eat quickly." She dropped her head to speak to her unborn child, "Slow down, *Pequeño*."

Omar and Sebastian giggled.

Ivana continued, "And your sister, Aimee?"

Tanner stared straight ahead at the road.

"My sister was in a bad," he sighed, "situation."

Ivana reached out and rubbed his shoulder. "We know, Tanner. Our mom told us. She can no longer talk, correct?"

Tanner nodded.

Sebastian interjected, "Yes, Tanner. We know. We are going to learn sign language."

Omar shouted excitedly, "We already learned this!"

He turned his open hand towards his mouth and then pressed his fingers to his thumb. He then made a fist, raised his index finger, and tapped his open palm against the raised finger.

Tanner laughed, "Y'all learning the insults first?"

Ivana chuckled, "Yep!"

Omar responded with his deepest, scratchy voice, "It means *shut up, fool!*"

Sebastian asked, "What about the farm and the animals?"

"Oh yes, Sebas! There are horses, pigs, chickens, cattle, dogs, barn cats," Tanner boasted.

"What about fish? Do you have fish?" Omar

replied excitedly.

Ivana reclined her seat. She was tired after eating. She closed her eyes.

Tanner replied to Marcito, "Not yet, buddy, but there is a lake close to the farm."

"Tell me about the horses, Tanner. Can I learn to ride a horse?" Sebastian interjected.

"Well, I think we . . . " Tanner paused when he heard Ivana snoring.

The boys chuckled.

"Go on, Tanner; tell us everything about the farm," Sebastian encouraged. He grabbed Moona from his little brother's lap and held onto her tightly.

34

Ivana's heart filled with joy as she watched her son talking with his grandmother. They were in the country surrounded by peach trees. Ivana was swinging from a tire attached to a very old scrub oak tree. It was a late afternoon in early summer. Her mother wore a sunflower-patterned dress and a peach-colored rose in her hair. Ivana's son was seated on the grass with an open book. The skinny, dark-haired young boy wore a curious expression. Emilia was making a fabric rope basket while listening to her grandson.

"I don't understand this quote, grandma. *Our chief want is someone who will inspire us to be what we know we could be.*"

Emilia paused, smiled warmly at the boy, and said, "That is an interesting quote, Isaac. What don't you understand?"

"Well, if we know what we could be, what keeps us from becoming who we are?" the boy replied.

Emilia laughed deeply and looked at her daughter and winked. Ivana continued to look at the two of them, as she leaned her head against the rope. Her heart fluttered on listening to her son.

Isaac continued, "Maybe I can help people, grandma." He pulled a blade of grass from the lawn and placed it as a bookmark and closed the book.

"How so, *amor?*" his grandma asked. She lowered her head as she ran the fabric rope through her fingers.

Isaac stood and walked towards his mother; he had

a solemn expression on his face. The young boy held onto his mother tightly. A gust of wind rushed through the orchard, which startled Ivana. She released Isaac from her embrace. The boy tried to straighten his mother's hair with his fingers and noticed she was crying. He wiped the tears from his mother's face and looked into her eyes, and said, "Mama, I want to inspire people to become who they want to be."

Ivana choked, "To be what, Isaac? What do you think they want to be?"

"I think everyone needs to be their own King, mama."

Ivana gasped. Her arms flailed as she forced herself to wake up from the dream. It was dark. Tanner pulled into a small town somewhere in New Mexico. Ivana clutched her stomach. Her face was full of tears.

Sebastian reached forward to comfort his sister. He placed his hands on her shoulders, and said, "We are going to stay here tonight."

Ivana tried to straighten up and looked hurriedly

out the window.

She then turned to Tanner, and said, "I need to find

a bookstore."

35

They were just minutes away from the family

farm. Ivana was reading the Bible she'd purchased the

night before in New Mexico. She had opened the Bible to

the Book of Kings. She had one hand pressed against her

pregnant belly and the other on the corner of the page she

was reading.

Tanner was *listening* to the boys learn sign

language.

"Okay, Marcito, how do you say 'Nice to meet

you'?" Sebastian asked.

Omar moved his open palm across the palm of his other hand and away from his body.

"Nice," he said excitedly. "To meet," he continued, as he raised his index fingers while making a fist with each hand. He then pointed at his brother and shouted, "You!"

Tanner gasped, "We're here!" His face turned red with emotion.

Ivana closed her book and noticed Tanner's expression. She leaned over and touched his shoulder. "Awe, yes, Papa Tanner, we are here."

He was startled by the word '*papa*.' It was the first time she had said that to him, and it immediately changed his countenance. He moaned joyfully, "Awe, look at that—the peach trees have fruit on them!"

The long driveway was surrounded by peach trees in both directions.

Sebastian opened his car window and yelled,

"Yes!" He pumped his arms over his head.

Tanner turned sharply between a row of trees. The asphalt road changed to dirt. It was early afternoon in mid-June. Tanner stopped the car beneath the shade of one of the fruit trees. He opened the door and called, "Come on, kiddos, let's take a look at the unripe peaches. Tanner reached above his head and touched a piece of fruit.

Ivana chimed, "They smell amazing."

Omar was struggling to keep Moona in his arms.

"Let her go, Marcito," Tanner said softly, "it's okay; this is her new home now. Let her run."

Moona started running in circles; she was filled with happiness.

"I have so many wonderful memories on this farm," Tanner shared. "When my mother died, I would hide in this orchard and talk myself to sleep underneath the shade of these peach trees. When anger filled my heart after my sister's tragedy, the horses were my only friends." He picked up a handful of soil and gathered his thoughts.

"This place has always been my home. I feel love in every fruit, every animal, and even in all of its smells." He lifted the soil towards his nose, inhaled deeply, and then dropped the soil.

"That includes the cow poopie smells too!"

The kids laughed but remained silent.

Tanner clutched his chest. "So much has happened since I left for Las Vegas with my sister. I had spent every day with Aimee since her tragedy." He shook his head, and said, "I became a prizefighting champion, served on the decks of the *Obrien* . . ." He shook his head, muttering, "And even saved and took a man's life."

Ivana interjected immediately, "Don't say that! Don't say that! You didn't take his life, Tanner!" She shook him.

Tanner pressed his lips together. He held her

tightly. "I'm sorry, Ivana," he choked.

He continued his thoughts privately.

"So much has happened. I met Elmer. My guardian angel opened the way for me to meet my Emilia. I married the love of my life, lost the love of my life, and now am fathering three of the most precious souls that have graced my journey."

Omar and Sebastian, always quick to hug, clutched Tanner's waist. Moona leaned her paws against his leg.

They were suddenly interrupted by the sound of a motorcycle that was fast approaching. A woman with long, wavy blonde hair, wearing muddy denim jeans and a soiled white T-shirt was riding the bike. An open mouth with bright red lips was tattooed on her bicep. Her helmet and shield covered her face. She stopped just in front of Tanner and the kids. The woman appeared startled and was breathing heavily.

Tanner released Ivana from their embrace. The

kids stood behind their papa. Tanner asked, "Can I help you?"

The biker put her kickstand into position. She lifted herself from the bike, leaned forward, and removed her helmet. She pushed her hair back and said, "Yes, you owe me a hug."

It was Aimee.

36

"Aimee! What happened?" Tanner turned pale.

His sister laughed, and said, "Well . . . " she stuck

out her tongue, and added, "I got me one of these."

Tanner quipped, "My God, did you steal that from

one of our cows?"

Aimee punched his shoulder. "A new medical

procedure has restored my life, thank God," she exhaled.

"So much has happened to you, my brother. I can tell that

you're not the same. You are the man I always hoped you

would become. Look at all the blessings that surround

you."

She turned and faced Ivana, and said, "You must be Ivana."

They embraced each other.

"Oh heavens, you are close." Aimee stepped back and gently touched Ivana's stomach. "I can't wait to learn everything about you." She crouched towards her belly and whispered, "I can't wait to meet you too."

The boys hovered around Aimee's bike. She let out a laugh, which caused Moona to rush towards her. Aimee reached down and lifted Moona into her arms. "I don't know who this lovely angel is." She puckered her lips and blew her kisses. Then, Aimee returned her gaze to the boys, and said, "But these two handsome boys must be Sebastian and Omar. Do you know how to ride a motorcycle?"

The boys shook their heads.

"That's okay, I'll teach you!" Aimee replied.

They asked excitedly, "Really!?"

Tanner laughed, "Come here, boys, and give your Aunt Aimee a hug." Tanner turned to his sister, "Well, we have a lot of catching up to do. I want to know everything. Why didn't you call and tell me the good news?"

"Dad asks me that question nearly every day. I made him promise not to tell you." She was holding Omar while rocking back and forth. She kissed the top of his head, and said, "You boys are going to have so much fun here." She released Omar.

Aimee approached her brother and whispered into his ear, "I wanted to surprise you." She punched his arm again. Aimee started to shadow box Tanner, as she said, "Come on and give me your best shot!"

Tanner grinned, as he shook his head and told her, "Let's go see dad."

37

Six weeks later.

Aimee and Tanner were riding in a golf cart. She had a surprise to show him. They were at the edge of the property. Aimee stopped the cart and pointed towards the construction. "I bought Hugh Amerine's place," she said.

"Really? What do you plan on doing with it? What are you building?" Tanner asked excitedly.

"Well . . . " she leaned forward, clutched the wheel, and said, "I'm going to build a school—a school for battered children."

"How awesome is that!" Tanner grinned.

"I know, right? It will be a small school, at first.

They will live on the property. We'll only be able to

provide for eight kids, but . . . " she whispered, "if I can

make this a success, I plan on building more schools."

"Aimee, that is wonderful."

Tanner interrupted their conversation to answer the

phone. It was their dad.

"Yeah, PaPa?"

"Tanner, come quick!" he could hear screaming in

the background. "It's Ivana—the little one is ready!" he

shouted excitedly.

Aimee overheard the conversation and turned the

cart quickly. Her foot pressed the pedal to the cart floor. It

was the longest ride of Tanner's life. The minutes that

passed seemed like hours. Finally, they reached the steps

to the farmhouse and were greeted by the screams of a

newborn infant. They paused momentarily, laughed

ecstatically, and rushed towards the front door. This was not the first baby born in the old farmhouse. They had both been born in this house as well. They followed the sounds to Ivana's room. She was covered in sweat. Their father and Stacey were busy cleaning up. The boys stood on each side of the bed. The tiny, brown, hairy-headed boy rested against his mother's bosom, covered in a blue blanket—the same blanket that had covered Tanner years ago. He stopped crying when he heard footsteps approaching the bed. Tanner looked at Ivana and the precious little one. He kneeled at the side of the bed and rubbed the infant boy.

"What are you going to call him, Ivana?" Tanner whispered.

"Well, I've already named him," Ivana said proudly.

Anxious to hear the answer, Stacey and Kenny stopped and put their arms around each other.

She kissed the boy's cheek, and said, "This is Isaac."

"Oh, what a beautiful name," Aimee and Tanner chimed.

Ivana pulled the blanket to cover some of Isaac's exposed neck, and Tanner's father placed a beanie on his head.

"Thank you, Great-Grandpa," she giggled. "Yes," Ivana continued, "wait until the world learns of my son's journey. It's no coincidence, Papa Tanner, that we are here at this farm and with you. Isaac has been burdened with a great task. I have seen it in my dreams, and you will be his teacher."

Tanner joked, "Yes, I might be able to give him a few tips about journeys."

Tanner's father laughed, and quipped, "Well, my wayward son, as long as that tip includes returning home."

Made in the USA
Monee, IL
03 February 2024

52277972R00184